I0546112

BEYOND PUCKERBRUSH

BY

C. DEANNE ROWE

Beyond Puckerbrush
by C. Deanne Rowe

Published by Citrine Group, L.L.C.
Des Moines, IA

Cover by Sterling Design Studios

First Printing:

ISBN-10: 978-1-946122-36-0
ISBN-13/EAN-13: 978-1-946122-36-0

Printed in the United States of America

DEDICATION

I fell in love with the characters of Puckerbrush. They became family even as their story venture beyond Puckerbrush. I can say I'm going to miss writing their stories. I can only hope they will all continue to talk to me and there will be another story to the Puckerbrush Series.

PROLOGUE
1960

"You have to take him. I can't provide for a child by myself." Penelope Johnson cried as she placed the swaddled baby on the worn church pew between her and Martin Wright.

"Surely you don't want to just give your baby away. I'm sure his father will return soon." Martin tried his best to calm her.

"I don't have any way to take care of him." Penelope sobbed.

Martin had been friends with Edward Dalton for years. Edward always returned from his revival tours. This time seemed different. Edward had been gone for several months longer than normal. Martin didn't have a good feeling about his return this trip, but he didn't want to let Penelope know.

The revivals Edward held during the summer months in different small towns were always a success and brought in enough money to pay for the church's expenses through the rest of the year. They agreed Martin would stay behind and take care of things. Mainly the congregation of the small church they started together. This time he hadn't heard anything from or about Edward for a while.

"I didn't ask for this child. Edward Dalton forced himself on me. I can't look at this baby without thinking of that night." Penelope broke down this time. Her body wracked with sobs; tears streamed down her youthful face.

Martin knew Penelope was the type of young woman Edward loved to counsel: fresh, innocent, and naive. He'd always feared something like this would happen. Edward taking advantage of one of these girls.

"The church will do everything we can to help you. We'll be the family you and your baby need during this trying time." Martin put his hand on her shoulder to comfort her, but he could only feel her body shake with each breath.

"We'll help you take care of your baby. I'll find a family that will take you and your baby in. A family that will give you a roof over your head and the help you need. We have a wonderful congregation that loves doing the Lord's work."

Martin knew there wasn't much the small church could do, but he would appeal to his congregation and maybe a few of the members would provide some help financially and spiritually for Penelope. If not, he would have to step up. He couldn't let Penelope or her baby suffer this way because of Edward.

"*You* can be this child's family." Penelope managed to speak.

Martin could see how serious she was when Penelope looked at him directly. Her eyes filled with desperation and fear.

"My father said I could return to live with them alone. He wouldn't be part of raising this child. I can't manage on my own. You have to understand. I didn't ask for this child. I just want to forget he was ever born." Penelope stood from the pew and ran out the door of the church leaving her baby behind.

Martin looked down at the baby snuggled in a tattered blanket sleeping so innocently, unaware of what was happening. This baby had no idea how he came to be. He had no idea the mother he would never know couldn't love him because of how he was created. He had no idea how much torment his father caused his mother and her family. It wasn't this blameless child's fault. Nothing was his fault. How could it be? An innocent child who now had no one. Martin picked up the sleeping baby and held him in his arms.

"I'm going to make sure you're taken care of and protected. I'll find a family who will raise you as their own. I promise I'll do my best to make sure you grow up and none of what has happened will be a part of your life."

Martin knew it was a promise he probably wouldn't be able to keep, but he would do his best. Edward Dalton was his friend and Martin knew he had a way of ruining the lives of everyone he knew. Martin wasn't going to let him ruin this innocent child's life if he could help it.

CHAPTER ONE

Present day

"We can't let them know we're who they're looking for." Joseph Wright slammed his hand down on his desk causing his Rolex to clang against the wood. "They'll ruin us if they find us. We'll have nothing left."

"You need to calm down, Joseph." Martin Wright pumped his hands up in down in front of him. "It's going to be difficult for them to connect us to Edward Dalton. I removed his name from any of the paperwork belonging to the church a long time ago when he never returned from holding his summer revivals."

"How do you know there isn't some kind of trail? Some way they can connect us to him. How do you know people in this town don't remember who he was?" Joseph asked through clenched teeth.

9

"I don't know that there isn't, but..." Martin carefully stood up from the chair he was occupying in front of Joseph's massive desk and held one finger in the air. "They're going to have to be excellent detectives to find out Edward Dalton was even connected to this church much less that he was your father."

"I've worked so hard to make this church the success it is." Joseph ran a hand down the front of his custom-made Italian suit jacket. "I'm the reason the pews are filled when the doors open. I'm the reason people flock to the church for messages of salvation. I'm the reason they give up their hard-earned money so freely. If it wasn't for me, this church would be nothing. I'm not sharing my success with anyone!" Joseph slammed his hand down on the desk one more time.

"Joseph, you have to stay calm. I'll take care of this just like I've taken care of everything since the day your mother left you with me. I've done everything in my power to protect you since you were a baby. I'm not going to stop now."

"I hope not." Joseph growled.

Martin took his seat. He wasn't as young as he used to be so when problems like this presented themselves, he needed to calm himself.

He'd loved Joseph from the day he set eyes on him. Looking at Joseph now, he remembered the innocent baby wrapped in the tattered blanket left by his mother who couldn't love him the way he deserved. Martin couldn't bring himself to take him to the orphanage and leave him as an abandoned baby. Martin knew the day he decided to take him home he needed to protect him *for* and *from* life. When he took the baby home to his wife, she reluctantly agreed to make him part of their family. She also promised she would tell no one who his real father was. He also remembered he'd promised Joseph wouldn't find out anything about how he'd come to be. Then, several years ago, he realized he didn't have a choice.

Martin still asked forgiveness daily for his part in saving Joseph from scandal by using his biological son to submit DNA instead of Joseph's when one of the church members sued him for child support, naming Joseph as the father of her child. Martin knew he needed to tell Joseph the truth then so he would understand what he was doing and why. That time Martin was able to save Joseph from humiliation and the church they'd built from ruin.

When Joseph's marriage ended due to an affair Joseph was having with one of the church members, Martin also saved him from humiliation by making sure Joseph's wife received a healthy settlement for her silence. Martin did his best to protect Joseph before. He needed to make sure he protected him from this also.

Now was different though. The stories and photos of Joseph's real father, Edward Dalton, making their way on television and in print, made it difficult for him to hide the truth from others. Joseph bore such a striking resemblance to his real father. His dark eyes and black hair made him stand out.

It was hard for Martin to convince people Joseph was his biological son because of Martin's red hair, pale complexion, and height. His wife having a darker complexion and coloring made it easier. Still, Joseph was much taller than Martin or any of the other Wright children. It was surprising the truth hadn't made its way out.

"I'll have the lawyers look over everything again and make sure there's no connection at all with Edward Dalton," Martin said.

"Make sure they check everything!" Joseph exclaimed. "Every nook and cranny. I don't want them to miss anything. Do you understand?"

Looking into Joseph's eyes as he put his hands down on the desktop in front of him and leaned in toward him, Martin had never seen this look before. He wasn't sure whether he should feel sorry for Joseph or afraid. "I'll make sure of it, Joseph. I promise you."

"I don't know if I trust your promises. You lied to me more than half my life about where I came from. Now people I don't even know saying they're children and grandchildren of my biological father are a threat to my livelihood. They're a threat to what I've created." Joseph sat back in his chair and let out a huff.

"I could care less about Edward Dalton, but I'm not sharing any part of this church or the fortune I've built with any of them. I've worked too hard for all of this." Joseph stood from behind his desk, stretched his arms in the air and made a slow turn around his huge office which was decorated with the finest of leather, wood, and expensive artwork.

"I did what I thought was best for you, Joseph. Besides, maybe they don't want any part of this church or your fortune." Martin watched Joseph as he admired the possessions he felt were important to him.

"You don't know that!" Joseph exclaimed. "I've taken the small, insignificant church you and my biological father started and turned it into this mega church. I've given you and the rest of the family a nice life. One you would've never had if you didn't take me in. If it wasn't for me, none of you would have a dime to your names."

Martin felt a chill run through his body when he saw the look on Joseph's face. He'd done everything he could to keep the actions and traits of Edward Dalton from developing in Joseph. It became more and more obvious as Joseph got older, he was a product of an evil man. A man who would stop at nothing to get what he wanted. A man who cared about no one except himself.

Martin believed there was good inside him somewhere. The love and care he and his wife showed Joseph during his childhood had to outweigh some of the bad. Did all the wealth and expensive possessions Joseph provided them because of the church blind Martin to the truth?

Just like the day his mother, Penelope, left Joseph in the chapel snuggled in a tattered blanket, it was Martin's turn to protect him again. This time he needed to make sure he did everything he possibly could to make it happen because, at his age, this might be the last time he would be alive to make sure Joseph was protected.

CHAPTER TWO

"You've done a magnificent job, Berta." Abigail Stratford-Thompson tried to take in everything there was to see in the new Puckerbrush Museum, while Archer squirmed in her arms.

"Let me take Archer so you look around. Aunt Berta will make sure he's snuggled tight."

"Thanks, Berta. It's almost time for him to eat so I'm not sure how good he'll be for you." Abigail carefully placed Archer in Berta's waiting arms.

"If you have a bottle, I can feed him." Berta offered. "It'll give me some bonding time."

"He's still breastfeeding." Abigail scrunched up her nose.

"Aunt Berta can't help you out there." Berta swayed back and forth and talked in baby talk as she attempted to calm Archer.

17

"He seems to be pretty happy with you right now so I'm going to look around. I'll come feed him when he starts getting fussy." Abigail lightly touched Archer's arm before she walked toward the town map standing in the middle of the room that caught her eye. "This is so cool."

"Isn't it? Pam asked one of the suppliers of her home décor store to make that for us. I thought he did a great job." Berta whispered to the beat of the song she was singing as she swayed back and forth trying to keep Archer happy.

"I love the way the name of all the shops are listed and it highlights what people should see while they're visiting Puckerbrush. I would've loved to have something like this when I visited for the first time." Abigail ran her hand across the map.

"I remember that day you came to Puckerbrush and checked into the Puckerbrush Motel just like it was yesterday." Berta smiled.

"So do I." Abigail turned and looked at Berta so lovingly holding Archer in her arms. Her grey hair pulled back in her classic French knot, her reading glasses hanging from a chain around her neck and wearing a dress that flattered her figure. Since Archer was born, Abigail felt good if the clothes she chose in the morning matched. Berta was always pulled together looking as if she had just stepped out of the salon.

"Did I ever tell you that you reminded me of a character in the book I'm writing?" Abigail asked.

"No, you didn't!" Berta exclaimed with surprise. "Why didn't you, or should I say Leeza McBride, tell me?"

"I'm still working on the story, but you have a main part in the book. I'll make sure you're the first to read it." Abigail winked at Berta.

"Even before Martha? I would love that. Martha, not so much." Berta shook her head and stuck her bottom lip out. "I also remember thinking what a good match you were going to be for our Matthew. He needed someone like you in his life."

"How did you know I would be a match for Matthew? You didn't even know me." Abigail asked.

19

"I'm a good at reading people. It comes from years of greeting people who stay at the Puckerbrush Motel. I could tell you were a good person. A person with a big heart. You were also single and very pretty. I knew once Matthew saw you, all the pieces of his life were going to fall into place." Berta looked down at Archer and smiled. "Matthew has given a lot to Puckerbrush and he lost a lot when his parents died in their house fire. He deserves to have someone like you in his life. A big city girl who keeps him on his toes." She laughed and swayed as Archer began to stir.

"I'm glad you could see it because it was touch and go there for a while for us. Once he learned the truth about his past, I almost lost him. I didn't even know if I could save our relationship." Abigail remembered the day she stopped to say goodbye. She was sure she was leaving Puckerbrush for good until Matthew changed his mind and asked her to stay. "Thank God I didn't lose him."

"Look at this beautiful baby you two have because you were meant to be together and, another plus, Puckerbrush has you also."

"And I have Puckerbrush and all the people who are such a big part of my life to help Matthew and I raise Archer. I'm a very lucky person and Archer's a very lucky little boy." Abigail placed her hand across her heart.

"We're the lucky ones. Believe me." Berta insisted.

"Before we both start crying, let's get back to the museum. I know how organized you are, Berta, and I know you're keeping a list of everyone we need to thank for all their work here in the museum."

"Of course. I wouldn't have it any other way."

Abigail noticed the desks where Eldon and Sister Angelica worked when they were publishing the *Puckerbrush Newspaper* were moved against the walls instead of being out in the middle of the room. The wooden floors had been refinished; the windows cleaned. She was amazed how much work was done to prepare the old *Puckerbrush Newspaper* building to become the Puckerbrush Museum. No matter how much cleaning or redecorating was done, Eldon was still here. She could feel him in every inch of the building.

Running her hand along the locked, wooden display case that held important pieces of history belonging to everyone in Puckerbrush, Abigail wiped away a tear.

The journals belonging to Eldon, Sister Angelica, and Eldon's daughter, Mary, were locked behind glass for everyone in town to see. These journals held so much history of Puckerbrush even if they were written by only three people. Feelings of hope, fear, heartbreak, and love filled the pages which years from now the people who read them would have a hard time understanding.

Abigail touched the crucifix she wore around her neck which Eldon made sure she had before he died. Images of him lying in the hospital bed barely able to breath flooded her memory, him making sure she knew the combination to the safe holding these journals was inscribed on the back.

Looking down the long row of shelves to where the safe Eldon hid behind stacks of books was located in the wall, Abigail saw it was still there and exposed for everyone who visited to see. Only she and Matthew knew the combination. She hadn't decided what to do with this information. Matthew mentioned turning it into a time capsule. She liked the idea of leaving something for future generations to discover. Maybe it would be Archer. Maybe it would be his children. The idea was intriguing.

The photos she'd taken of the people and the town during the Puckerbrush Centennial Celebration lined the walls of the museum. Some of the photos which before were hung on the wall of the Puckerbrush Café now hung here.

There was a picture of Sister Angelica which Uncle Charles discovered during the remodeling Eldon's old home. It had been tucked away safely in a closet by Eldon. It must have been taken at the orphanage a few years after Sister Angelica found Eldon abandoned along a dirt road. It was one of only a few photos Eldon kept. She and Matthew kept the photos Eldon placed beside his bed of his wife, and daughter, Mary, Matthew's biological grandmother. They belonged on the shelf with the few remaining family photos in Matthew's possession.

The stories of all these people from Puckerbrush were frozen in time in these photos which brought Abigail to tears as she felt she knew each one of them personally. Her life changed so much when she visited here to write an article about the Puckerbrush Centennial Celebration. Instead, she found out she loved and belonged in Puckerbrush.

The shelves holding binders of the old newspapers going back to when Sister Angelica started the newspaper were labeled and organized. A cross reference of what all the shelves held was placed on the end of each one. So many years of history lined these shelves.

"The kids are going to get so much out of this place." Abigail kept moving down each of the rows. "That's what Eldon would've wanted. He would've wanted the kids to know all they could about the town where they live. I know he would be so happy with what you've done, Berta."

"That mean so much to me." Berta cleared her throat as her voice began to crack. "Did you talk to your publisher to see if you could put some of your Leeza McBride books on display? I'm sure visitors would love to have an autographed book from a famous author. It would be a surprise when they visit. I'm sure the book with me as one of the characters will be the most requested one."

"I'm sure it will be." Abigail laughed. "I'm working on it like I'm working on my next book. Leeza needs to get her act together. Things have been put on hold since Archer was born. I don't know what I did with my time before he arrived."

"I can understand." Berta continued to sway back and forth. "When you need a break, you just call Aunt Berta and she'll come help out. Right, Archer?"

"I'm sure Archer's going to love spending time with his Aunt Berta and here in the Puckerbrush Museum." Abigail also knew how much there was for him to learn about Puckerbrush. The town where his life began.

CHAPTER THREE

"Hello ladies." Martha waited inside the door of the Puckerbrush Café, dressed in jeans with her blouse tucked in showing her tiny waist and perfect figure, holding her arms out for a hug.

"Hi, Martha." Berta gave her a quick hug.

"How are you?" Abigail shifted the car seat holding baby Archer into the opposite hand and gave Martha a hug with the free one. "I don't know how you ladies do it. You're always so pulled together. Tell me I'm going to be that way again."

"Nonsense," Martha replied. "You look beautiful as always. I'd love to have that natural beauty again and not have to work so hard. Let me see that baby." Martha leaned down, smiling as her voice rose in pitch. "Hello Archer. I'm so happy to see you. You know you're going to be the star of the party this afternoon."

"I'm sure if he doesn't get fed soon, no one is going to want to be around him." Abigail laughed. "I'm going to borrow one of your back rooms and feed him."

"Can I hold him and walk back with you? I haven't gotten to see him or you for a few days." Martha asked. "I need to catch up on my hugs."

"Sure." Abigail set the car seat and the diaper bag down on the closest table and unbuckled Archer. She carefully picked him up out of the seat, gave him a kiss and then handed him to Martha.

"Oh, he's growing so fast." Martha said placing a few kisses on his cheeks as Archer began to fuss. "All right sweetie. Your momma's going to feed you."

"I know the party isn't going to start for a little while so you're going to have to come back out here and let Berta tell you about the kids at the museum today. It was so much fun." Abigail picked up the car seat and diaper bag and began walking with Martha toward the back room.

"I'm guessing they enjoyed it?" Martha asked.

"They had so much fun." Abigail smiled, remembering the kids running around pointing out everything they liked. "And your cookies were a huge hit."

"I like hearing that. What kid doesn't love a cookie? Archer's going to love my cookies and apple pie when he gets old enough." Martha gave him another kiss on the cheek.

"All of the kids asked good questions and it seemed like they were really interested in learning about Puckerbrush. I think the museum is a wonderful addition to the town. The teachers mentioned they were going to find a way to fit a visit to the museum into their day every week or so. They just have to walk the class across the park and they're there."

Abigail's thoughts went back to a few days after Eldon passed away. She'd sat outside the newspaper building on the bench where Eldon always spent his days watching everyone in town go about their business. She realized he had the perfect view of Puckerbrush and all that was happening in the town. The school was across the park. The sheriff's office was down the street. The Puckerbrush Café was right across the street which was where she first saw him. It was as if he was the protector of Puckerbrush. Life was normal if Eldon was sitting on his bench.

"I'm so happy you came up with the idea to turn the old *Puckerbrush Newspaper* building into a museum. It was a terrific idea for that building. I'm sorry I couldn't get away this morning to be there with you two. I peeked in a few times when Berta was doing some decorating though." Martha bounced Archer in her arms to keep him occupied while Abigail got settled in the chair then she reluctantly handed him off.

"I'll be out as soon as he's finished nursing. I'm hoping he goes to sleep for a little while." Abigail crossed her fingers.

"If he doesn't, we'll just pass him around until he's worn out. I'll see you when you're done." Martha walked out of the room closing the door behind her.

Abigail settled Archer in place. As he snuggled in and began nursing, she laid her head back on the chair, closed her eyes and began plotting scenes in her head for the book she was writing. Being in the museum this afternoon seemed to spark her creativity and also her memories of Eldon.

****

"He must have been tired. He fell right to sleep. I left him in the little pack n play you set up in the room. I can't believe you did that for him." Abigail gave Martha a hug.

"Before you thank me, you should know it was for a very selfish reason." Martha smiled. "I thought if he had a place to sleep, you two would come by and visit more often."

"I see. I guess I'm going to have to put one up at the motel." Berta placed her hands on her hips and sighed.

"You know, you both are always welcome to come to the house and spoil him all you want. Archer and I are always happy to see you." Abigail placed the baby monitor she packed in her bag down on an empty table and sat down in the closest chair. "Did Berta fill you in on the party for the kids at the museum?"

"She did. She told me how all kids enjoyed the pictures you took of the Puckerbrush Centennial parade," Martha said. "There are so many memories there for all of them."

"They tried to find themselves, their friends, and family in the pictures. It was so cute." Berta laughed.

"Hi ladies." Matthew walked through the front door of the café heading straight for Abigail and gave her a kiss.

"I guess we know who rates here, Berta." Martha motioned toward Matthew and Abigail.

"I remember the day when we were the first women in the room to get a hug and kiss from Matthew." Berta crossed her arms in front of her body.

"Come on. You ladies know you're special to me." Matthew gave each of them a bear hug then turned back to Abigail. "Where's Archer?"

"He's asleep in the back room. I just fed him. He was pretty exhausted so he fell right to sleep." Abigail yawned.

"It looks like Mom's pretty exhausted also. Are you sure you want to stay for the party? We can go home if you want." Matthew offered.

"Are you joking?" Abigail exclaimed. "This is the first time I've been out of the house all week. I'm looking forward to seeing everyone who helped with the museum and thanking them for everything they've done."

Matthew put his hands up in the air. "You got it. I think it's great you guys are throwing everyone who helped a party. Even though I didn't do anything to help, I'm looking forward to the food. There's going to be pie right?"

Martha glared at Matthew with one of her you-can't-be-serious looks. "You really think I'd have a party and not include some of my apple pie?"

"I stand corrected." Matthew laughed. "I think I'll go back and check on my son before I get in any more trouble."

"Give him a kiss for me." Berta yelled behind him.

Matthew held a thumb up in the air as he made his way down the hallway toward the back room.

Abigail stood up from the chair as guests began to arrive. She glanced around the café which was perfectly decorated for a party. "What can I help with, Martha?"

"You and Berta can greet the guests. I'll go finish setting all the food and drinks on the tables." Martha disappeared into the kitchen.

"Welcome everyone." Berta put an arm around Abigail's waist. "Abigail and I are happy you all could make it."

****

"That went well." Berta began picking up some of the empty plates and glasses that were left behind on the tables, stacking all of them carefully so she could carry them to the kitchen.

"Yes, it did." Abigail helped by wiping off the tables as Berta cleared off the dishes. "I'm glad everyone could come. They did so much to help us out. I mean everything that was special to them, now the whole town can share. I'm always amazed by the people of Puckerbrush. We wouldn't have been able to open the museum without them."

"Me too." Berta smiled. "Where did Matthew sneak off to?"

"He went back to the office. I think once he had his fill of Martha's apple pie, he was happy." Abigail laughed. "He's been saving space for pie all week."

"I'm sure he's busy. I'm glad he stuck around long enough to say hi to everyone." Berta balanced a stack of dirty dishes and began to walk toward the kitchen.

"You ladies don't have to do that. I'll take care of it. Why don't you sit down and relax?" Martha brought an empty container to carry away all the dishes.

"We don't mind helping. I think the one who did the cooking shouldn't have to do the cleaning." Berta placed the handful of dishes she was holding in the container.

"I've been meaning to ask you if you and Charles are settling into the new house?" Abigail placed a few glasses in the container Martha was holding as well.

"It's been going well. All the remodeling was done before the wedding. There are just a few things that need to be tweaked. Charles loves the way all the changes we made came out." Martha grinned.

"What about you?" Abigail tilted her head sideways trying to interpret Martha's reply. She knew her uncle had been single for long enough he might forget to ask Martha's opinion. "Do you like how they turned out?"

"I do. Your uncle has great decorating skills. I would've never thought of some of the ideas he did. He surprises me every day." The warmth of her smile lit her eyes.

"I'm so glad you two are happy." Berta stacked some more dishes in the container.

"Me too. It's so wonderful to see Uncle Charles settled and so happy. I also love having him so close. I would never have imagined him living in Puckerbrush instead of Chicago. I guess it took the right woman to make it happen." Abigail smiled.

I'm glad he made you promise he could perform your wedding ceremony." Martha grinned. "I would've never met him otherwise."

"Me too." Abigail agreed. "What about John and Emily? Have they found a place to live? I know the backroom John was living in isn't enough room for both of them."

"I didn't tell you?" Martha asked. "They're moving into my house."

"How nice." Berta clapped her hands together.

"That is great." Abigail agreed. "I'm sure they're happy to have a place to move to. Last I heard they were still looking. I know there's not that much available in Puckerbrush. That worked out perfectly, Martha."

"Yes, it did. The house is paid for. I didn't want to sell it or have it sit empty when I moved in with Charles, so I asked them if they wanted to live there. I thought it would give them a chance to decide what they wanted to do on a more permanent basis."

"How's her mother?" Abigail's concern showed in her expression.

"She's doing the same. Emily and John try to go visit her every week." Martha's tone turned somber.

"That's good, isn't it?" Abigail asked. "I mean for Emily. I remember her saying her mother doesn't know who she is most of the times she visits."

"You're right, Abigail. I just hate that Emily's having to deal with this at her young age. She should be enjoying her life and looking forward to what's ahead. But since her father just walked out, she's the only one left to care for her mother. She took on so much responsibility. I'm amazed at how well she handles it all."

"She's never heard from her father again?" Abigail couldn't imagine having a parent out there that you had no contact with.

"Not that Emily has mentioned. She came home from school one day and he was waiting for her with all his things packed. I guess he couldn't handle what was happening with his wife." Martha shrugged her shoulders.

"I'm so glad you're here to help them," Berta said.

Martha stopped for a moment. "I remember when I lost my husband. I would've given anything for someone to talk to or lean on. I want to be that person for John and Emily if I can."

Abigail walked over and gave Martha a hug. "You're that person for all of us." The noise of Archer stirring over the monitor interrupted. "I'm being paged."

"Let me go get him." Martha giggled. "I love to be the first person a waking baby sees. They're always so happy."

"Go ahead." Abigail motioned toward the hallway. "I'm sure he needs his diaper changed. You're welcome to do that also. Everything you need is in the diaper bag."

Martha smiled as she trotted down the hallway toward the room.

Abigail shook her head. "Archer doesn't stand a chance of not being spoiled."

CHAPTER FOUR

"My mother and I would make these once a month on Saturday night. We would let them rise all night then bake them Sunday morning while we were getting ready for church. It was always a special treat and a reason to spend time together." Emily rubbed her fingers down the piece of paper before laying it down on the counter of the Puckerbrush Café for Martha to see.

"I found it in a recipe box packed away in one the boxes from my mother's house." Emily dropped her hands in her lap. "I was in such a bad place when I was going through my mother's things and packing them away, all I cared about was putting almost everything in boxes in case I needed to sell the house and move. I only left out the bare essentials." Emily remembered thinking she was tucking everything away like she felt she'd done with her mother when she placed her in the Alzheimer's care facility.

She and John moving into Martha's house after their wedding gave her a reason to finally go through everything. She didn't realize how many memories each of the boxes held.

"Mom told me this recipe was handed down to her from her grandmother. I always felt so close to people I never met when we would make them."

"I can see that." Martha, sitting on the barstool next to her, rubbed her hand down Emily's back as she fought back tears. "I'm glad you found it."

"Me too." Emily turned to look at Martha. "I was wondering if you would make them with me sometime. I thought I would surprise John. He's always cooking for me so I thought I would do something for him. Maybe share some of my past with him."

"Are you sure you want me to make them with you?" Martha placed her hand against her chest.

"Yes." Emily nodded.

"I'd be honored to." Martha smiled. "What if we do it now? The café's not busy and John's taking a short nap in the back room after the lunch rush. We can make them and you can take them home to let them rise. If you want to bake them at home in the morning and bring them with you, we'll have them for breakfast."

"I like that idea. I know the perfect place to keep them so John won't see them." Emily looked off in the distance as she contemplated her plan.

"I'm so happy you asked me to help you." Martha smiled. "It means a lot you feel close enough to me you can share this kind of memory."

"I feel very lucky you came along with my marriage to John. Something was missing in my life after I put my mom in the Alzheimer's facility. I feel like John and you have filled that missing spot. It's like I finally found where I belong." Emily put her arm around Martha's waist.

Martha wiped a tear from her cheek and hugged Emily tightly. "We better get started then before both of us start blubbering."

"I'm ready." Emily patted the tears from her cheeks.

Taking the piece of paper from Emily's hand, Martha read the list of ingredients. "We have everything we need. I'll gather it all together while you put on this apron." She stood and walked through the door of the kitchen, Emily following behind. Martha laughed as she took an apron off the wall hook behind her. "I have a feeling both of us are going to need one of these or we're going to have flour all over us."

"Do we have to?" Emily asked as she scrunched up her nose. "That was the fun part of making them, seeing how much flour we could get on our clothes."

"You don't have to wear one, but I am and you're cleaning up when we're done." Martha pointed in Emily's direction then reached for the flour and sugar on the counter and placed them on the metal table.

"That doesn't sound like fun." Emily slipped the apron over her head. "Do you trust me to do some of the kneading of the dough? Mom would always give me a small piece of dough and make me watch her so I could learn. She always told me when I was old enough, I could knead instead of her. We never got there."

Martha glanced at Emily and winked. "I think you're old enough to do the kneading."

"Great." Emily clapped her hands together. "I did get to mix the cinnamon and sugar together that gets sprinkled on the dough after it's rolled out. Mom always melted the butter while I did that part. It's been so many years since I've done this but it feels like yesterday."

"You can do whatever you want. I'll just be here for support. How's that?" Martha asked as she looked for the cinnamon and a package of yeast.

"Perfect." Emily walked behind the table where Martha placed all the ingredients. She began carefully measuring out everything just as it was written on the recipe as Martha gathered the rest. The memories were all coming back. Her heart was full.

****

"Okay." Martha placed a clean kitchen towel over the pan of cinnamon rolls. "These are ready for you to take home, let rise, and then bake them in the morning."

Emily put the recipe in her jeans pocket and started to pick up the pan from the table then stopped. "Thank you so much, Martha. It was fun baking with you." Emily gave her a quick hug.

"It's my pleasure." Martha whispered. "I had fun baking with you. I'm so glad you asked me."

"I'll take this pan home and hide them." Emily picked the pan up from the table. "I can't wait to taste them in the morning."

"Oh, wait." Martha opened the refrigerator door and pulled out a container. "Don't forget the icing."

"I'm glad you remembered. I would have forgotten it. I'll make sure they're cooled off a little before I ice them." Emily took the container. "I'll see you in the morning."

43

"You would've forgotten what?" John asked as he walked through the side door of the kitchen rubbing his eyes.

"Nothing." Emily quickly answered.

"What are you two up to?" the tone of John's voice lowered as he looked around the room. "I can tell when the two of you are up to no good."

"We're up to good this time." Emily set the pan down on the table and walked toward John.

When she got close enough, John reached out and pulled her close. "It's nice to see you." He kissed her lightly.

"It's nice to see you too, but I've got to go. I'll see you at home later." Emily smiled, picked up the pan, and began to make her way out of the kitchen.

"Why are you in such a hurry?" John held his hand up in the air. "What's in the pan? Wait around and I'll make you dinner."

"I've got to go. See you later. I love you." Emily hurried out the front door of the cafe to her car and placed the pan carefully on the seat next to her. "I can't wait to see how they taste."

****

"Delicious." Martha took another bite of her cinnamon roll.

44

"They are." Charles agreed. "I don't think I've ever had a roll this good and I've had a lot of cinnamon rolls." He patted his stomach as he laughed.

"I can't believe you made these for me." John put his arm around Emily and pulled her close.

She laid her head on his shoulder. "I wanted to do something nice for you because you're always doing something nice for me." Emily leaned up and kissed his cheek.

"I love you too." John smiled.

"What do you think about putting them on the menu of the Puckerbrush Café?" Martha waited for Emily to answer.

"You really want to put them on the menu?" Emily wanted to make sure she heard Martha correctly.

"Yes, I do. I think they would be a great addition. I've made cinnamon rolls but nothing this good." Martha took another bite. "Now that Charles is around to help us out in the kitchen, we have the extra hands."

"I agree. I don't know what it is that makes them taste so good, but I think Mom's right. They would do really well with our breakfast crowd." John agreed.

"I think my mother would be happy if she knew they were going to go on your menu." Emily said. "I'm sure you could probably add your touch, Martha, and they would be even better."

"I don't know if they could be any better." Martha smiled. "In fact, they might outsell my apple pie."

"No way." Emily exclaimed. "I did have an idea though."

"What's that?" Martha asked.

"What if we add your apple pie filling in a batch and see how they come out. I mean apple pie cinnamon rolls sound really good to me." Emily glanced at John while she waited to see what everyone thought.

"Why don't we try it and see if we all like it? I think you might be on to something, Emily." Martha patted Charles on the shoulder. "You want to help us? You and John can get your hands dirty too."

"I'm the cook around here, not the baker." John held his hands up in the air. "I'm going to pass and leave the baking up to you guys."

"I'll give it a shot." Charles said. "I'm game for anything."

"And that's what I love about you." Martha gave Charles a hug.

46

"Do you think you could get away from the café for a few hours this afternoon?" Emily looked at John.

"Possibly. What's up?" John asked.

"I thought maybe we could take one of these rolls to my mother." Emily paused. "I've been thinking about her a lot since I've been unpacking the boxes of her stuff and now the rolls."

John put his arm around her and pulled her close. "If you want to stick around and help out, of course I can get away right after the lunch rush. I think your mother would love one of these rolls. Maybe it'll bring back some memories for her."

"Thank you. I was hoping the same thing." Emily put her head on John's shoulder and closed her eyes. "From your mouth to God's ears."

CHAPTER FIVE

"Hi, Mom." Emily moved closer to where her mother sat beside the only window in her room enjoying the view. John had put a bird feeder outside her mother's window. He thought it would give her a way to pass some time.

Dorothy Clayton turned to look at Emily and John and smiled. Emily squeezed John's hand hoping he'd noticed. It had been a long time since her mother greeted her with a smile.

"Are you enjoying the view, Mrs. Clayton?" John asked as they moved closer to her chair. "It's really a beautiful day and the birds are busy."

"We brought you something." Emily put the cinnamon roll Martha carefully placed in a plastic container on the table beside her mother's chair. "I thought you might enjoy it with your dinner tonight."

Dorothy picked up the roll and held it up to her nose then turned it around in her hand, inspecting each side. "I love cinnamon rolls." She paused for a moment as if she was in thought. "My daughter and I make the most wonderful cinnamon rolls. We have so much fun making them together. Her job is to mix the cinnamon and sugar just right and then sprinkle it all over the rolled-out dough after I've brushed on the melted butter." Dorothy held her hand up as if she was sprinkling the mixture.

Emily wanted to tell her mother that she was her daughter. *She* was the little girl she was remembering, but she didn't. She watched and listened to Dorothy tell her story.

"She always wants to knead the dough, bless her heart, so I always give her a little pinch and let her knead that while I knead the rest of the dough. I know her little arms aren't strong enough to handle the kneading that needs to be done." A slight smile crossed Dorothy's face. "I always tell her she needs to learn the proper way to knead the dough because kneading is the secret to why they taste so good."

Emily's heart was breaking. She could tell this memory made her mother happy. She wanted this moment to last forever. A moment she hadn't experienced in the longest time. Her mother was actually remembering her and their time together.

"We make them on Saturday night. She loves coming down the next morning and seeing how much they've risen." Dorothy laughed. "The smile on her little face is so beautiful." The happiness showing on Dorothy's face lasted a little longer as she continued. "We then bake them as we get ready for church and always enjoy one before church and another after dinner that night. This one looks and smells just like the ones we made."

She waited for her mother to keep going, but it seemed she was lost in this memory. She wanted to hang onto this moment for a little longer. A tear dripped down her cheek and fell on her hand. Emily was so lost in her mother remembering she didn't realize she was crying. Glancing at John, she saw tears falling down his face also. He took her hand. "She remembers me." Emily whispered. "She remembers me."

Dorothy kept a tight hold on the cinnamon roll as she laid her head back on her chair with a smile on her face and closed her eyes. Before long she was asleep.

Emily took a small blanket from the end of the bed and placed it over her mother's lap then kissed her forehead and whispered. "I love you, Mom."

She took John's hand and smiled. This feeling of a having a mother who knew who she was wasn't going to leave her for a long time.

****

Pulling into one of the parking spots in front of the Puckerbrush Café, Emily opened her car door and took a few deep breaths before walking to the front door of the café. She needed to see John and talk to him. She wasn't sure how she was going to tell him or what she was going to say. She just needed him to hold her and tell her everything was going to be all right.

"Hi, Emily." Martha greeted her as she walked through the door. "Matthew and I were just talking about you."

"These cinnamon rolls are the best thing I've had since the last time I had a slice of Martha's apple pie." Matthew turned and held up his last bite of cinnamon roll.

"Is John around?" Emily asked. She couldn't say anything else.

Martha walked from behind the counter to meet her. "Is everything all right?"

"I don't know. I need to talk to John," was all Emily could say.

"He's in the kitchen. Come with me." Martha took her hand. "I'll make sure he knows you're here."

Emily held on to Martha's hand as she walked through the kitchen doorway. The moment she spotted John she started sobbing.

"What's wrong Emily." John ran up to her and took her in his arms.

She felt his arms wrap tightly around her. She needed that feeling right now. Emily tried to speak, but wasn't able to get the words out. All she could do was cry. She wanted to tell him, but she couldn't. Not right now. Trying to take a few deep breaths, Emily finally was able to say one word. "Mom."

"What about your mother?" John asked.

"Your mother? Is she all right?" Martha asked as she stood on the other side of Emily with her hand on her back. "Take your time. You can tell us what's wrong whenever you can. We'll be right here. We're not going anywhere."

"Is everything okay?" Matthew asked as he walked through the kitchen door.

"Emily's going to tell us when she can." Martha shrugged as she looked at Matthew.

"We just went to see her mother yesterday." John explained. "We took her one of the cinnamon rolls Emily made. It was a great visit. Her mother remembered when she and Emily would make the cinnamon rolls together. Emily came away with a good feeling about her mother. It was great. I don't know what happened between then and now."

"She's dead." Emily finally managed to speak. Her body was shaking with each breath she took.

"What?" John asked as he took her in his arms again.

"Oh, honey. I'm so sorry." Martha rubbed her back as John held her.

"I'm really sorry to hear that, Emily." Matthew shook his head. "I don't mean to run but I've got to get to work. I'll call later and find out how things are. Just remember; Abigail and I'll do whatever you need to help you out, Emily. She'll be so sad to hear the news."

"Thank you." Emily managed to whisper.

"Thanks, Matthew. I'll talk to you later." Martha gave him a quick hug before he walked out the kitchen door.

"Come sit down. I'll get you a glass of water or would you rather have coffee?" Martha asked.

"I just want John." Emily's body shook as she spoke. "I want him to remind me how good yesterday was. How my mother remembered me. How she knew who I was. She knew I was her daughter and she remembered how much fun we had together. I want him to tell me that when she died, she remembered who I was." Emily began sobbing again.

"She did remember you." John hugged her tighter. "She knew exactly who you were. She remembered the two of you making cinnamon rolls together. She died knowing you were her daughter."

"Thank you." Emily whispered as she turned and looked at Martha. "Thank you for helping me make those cinnamon rolls so she would remember."

"You're welcome, Emily. I'm so sorry about your mother. John and I are here for you. Whatever it is you need. We love you and you don't have to go through this alone." Martha began to cry.

CHAPTER SIX

Emily knew exactly which dress and shoes she wanted to find. She could see her mother in them and she remembered how much her mother enjoyed wearing them to church on Sunday. Memories of her mother turning in circles after she'd come down the stairs and wait for Emily to tell her how pretty she looked flooded her thoughts. It was her favorite color, royal blue. She had the perfect pair of shoes to wear with it. Emily knew right where everything was in her mother's closet.

As she unlocked and began opening the front door of her mother's house, the fragrance of Italian food put her senses on alert. It had been at least two months since she'd been here. There shouldn't be cooking smells. She stopped right inside the doorway, took her cell phone from her jeans pocket and set her phone to dial emergency.

"Hello." Emily called out as she looked around to see if anything was out of place. "Is anyone here?"

Hearing footsteps coming down the stairway, she quickly backed up as she called 911.

"911. What's your emergency?" the female voice on the end of the line asked.

"I'm at my mother's house and someone's in there. My mother's deceased. No one should be in there." Emily tried to stay calm and began rattling off the address as she made her way back to her car. "Please send someone quick."

"Officers are on the way. Stay on the line with me if you can." The woman asked, "What's your name."

"Emily Clayton-Jackson. My mother, Dorothy Clayton, owns the house." Emily's heart raced. She placed her free hand on her chest as she took a few deep breaths and backed up close to her car. "She passed away a short time ago. There shouldn't be anyone in there."

"I understand, Emily." The woman interrupted her, but her voice was calm. "The officers will check it out when they get there. They should be there shortly. Just stay on the phone with me until they arrive and don't go in the house." The woman insisted.

Emily could hear the sirens in the distance. "I think I hear them coming."

"Make sure they see you, Emily. Let me know when you can see them."

"I can see them now." She waved her free hand as the police car came closer.

"When they address you, I'll hang up and you can talk to them. The officers have all the information you have given me."

"Emily Clayton-Jackson?" A nice-looking policeman in uniform got out of the squad car, his hand on his belt as he walked closer to her. His female partner joined him. Her blonde hair pulled back in a ponytail, sunglasses covered her eyes. "I'm Officer Smith. This is my partner Officer Timms. We understand you have an intruder."

"Yes." Relief flooded her as her heartrate began to slow down. "No one should be here. My mother is deceased. This is her house."

"Is the door unlocked?" Officer Smith asked.

"Yes, I unlocked it before I realized someone was in there. I heard footsteps on the stairs." Emily answered.

"You stay right here. We'll check it out." Officer Smith instructed her.

"Oh, you don't have to worry about that. I'm not moving." Emily leaned against her car for support.

"I'm going to hang up now." The 911 operator replied. "The officers will take care of everything."

"Thank you so much." Ending the call, she listened as the officers called out.

"Police. Is someone in here?"

Closing her eyes, she strained to hear an answer to the Officer's question. There was nothing except silence for what seems several minutes. Officer Smith's voice suddenly broke that silence.

"Stay where you are."

Emily stopped breathing for a few seconds as she waited, wishing she could see what was happening. Another male voice replied, but she couldn't make out what he was saying. She wanted to move closer so she could hear except she was almost glued to her car afraid whoever was in there would try to run. She needed to be able to escape.

Officer Timms suddenly appeared. "We've got a male who says this is his house. Would you come with me so we can settle this?" She motioned for Emily to join her.

"Is it safe?" Emily asked.

"Yes. My partner has him handcuffed." Officer Timms explained.

Emily walked with Office Timms to the front door of the house. When she walked through the doorway, she couldn't believe what she was seeing. Words failed her. She recognized the handcuffed man standing beside Officer Smith.

"Do you know this man?" Officer Timms asked. "Like I said before, he's telling us this is his house."

Emily began to speak in stutters. "Yes. I do know him. He's my father."

"Hello, Emily." The barefoot man dressed in jeans and a sloppy t-shirt said.

The sound of his voice telling her goodnight, calling her name from the bottom of the stairs echoed through her memories. How could this be that same man?

Officer Smith rubbed the back of his neck. "If this is your father, then he probably has the right to be here."

Emily couldn't take her eyes off the man who was standing next to Office Smith. What was left of his hair was messy, he was barefoot, handcuffed, and wearing a smug grin across his face. The past ten years had taken a toll on him.

"It's a long story, Officer Smith. He left my mother and I when she became sick. I haven't seen or heard from him in years. My mother died a short time ago. This was her house, not his. He has no right to be here." Her voice rose as old feelings of betrayal began to surface. She folded her arms across her body refusing to let him see her cry.

"I can understand why you think that, but he says his name is on the deed," Officer Smith replied.

"My mother had Alzheimer's and since he deserted her when her memory faded, the last thing we needed to worry about was taking his name off the deed. The house is paid for with no thanks to him. I have a power of attorney and I don't want him here." Emily stood firmly in place not moving a muscle.

"I've run his ID and he checks out. He *is* Henry Clayton." Office Smith held up what looked like a driver's license.

"I know who he is and yes, his name's Henry Clayton, but he doesn't belong here. He left years ago and this is not his home any longer." Emily insisted. "I want him out of here."

"It's okay, Officer." Henry Clayton finally broke his silence. "If you'll take these handcuffs off, I'll get my things and leave. Emily, we can talk about this sometime. I'm not planning to leave town."

"Is that all right with you?" Officer Smith motioned in Emily's direction when she didn't answer.

"As long as he leaves the house, it's fine." Emily snarled. "I can't make him leave town even though I would love to."

"We'll stay right here until you're done." Officer Smith unlocked the handcuffs and placed them back on his belt.

"Thank you." Attempting a half smile, she watched her father disappear up the stairway. Once he gathered his belongings and walked out the front door, she could go back to her life as it has been for the past ten years...fatherless.

CHAPTER SEVEN

"The thought of changing the locks never even crossed my mind." Emily played with the food on the plate John made for her. "I guess in a way I was hoping he would change his mind and come back. I can't even remember when I gave up on that idea."

"I can see how that would be the last thing you would think about." John put his arm around her shoulder. "I mean you were taking care of your mother and trying to finish college. You had so much on your plate at the time."

"I can't believe he just showed up thinking he could walk back into her house and make himself at home." Emily put her fork down on her plate and pushed it away from her on the table then stared out the window of the Puckerbrush Café.

"The thought of him being there almost makes me ill and the fact he had company. Sharing the house and my mother's bed with someone else."

"Do you know who was there with him?" John asked.

"No. I didn't even think about someone being there with him until I went through the house to clean up. When I found two wine glasses, two paper plates along with an empty pizza box on the kitchen counter, I knew he hadn't been there alone. I could tell two people slept in my mother's bed. I ripped the bedsheets off and threw them away." Emily sunk back in her chair and folded her arms across her body.

"Don't think about him. He's out of there. The officers made sure of that. And you've changed the locks so he can't get back in. I'll go back with you and we'll make sure everything's all right." John offered. "I knew I should've gone with you this time."

"I was just going to pick up clothes and leave. I didn't even think about someone being in the house. I've never felt scared or afraid while we were living there. This time was different though." Emily rested her head in her hands. "I don't ever want to see him again. As far as I'm concerned, he's dead just like my mother."

"I reached out to the lawyers we use for the café's business and they gave me a reference. She's checking into everything to make sure you can keep him out. I don't know enough about the legal side of all this to promise you anything. I can tell you the lawyer will do all she can to make sure he has no rights." John reached up and took her hand in his.

"Thanks for taking care of that. I wouldn't even know where to begin. I trusted my mother's lawyer friend to handle the legal side when Mother started getting worse. When he moved away, I never thought about finding a new lawyer. I thought everything was done. I guess I should've done more to protect her from him since he was heartless enough to walk out on her." Her father's image rose in Emily's mind, smiling as if he'd done nothing wrong.

"He not only walked out on her, but he also left you and left you to deal with everything. You did what you needed to do. You took care of your mother and yourself. It'll all work out. I'll be here to make sure of that." John squeezed her hand and smiled.

"I hope so. I just want him gone for good. I don't ever want to see his face again."

Was it the anger speaking or the hurt from remembering him walking out the door? Whatever it was, she wasn't going to let it take over. She determined to be strong like she had to be the day he left; no matter how hard it would be. She was going to take care of things just like she did then. This time there was John. John, Martha and all the other friends and family now in her life. This time she wasn't alone.

****

"Come here and give me that sweet baby." Martha put her arms out as Abigail walked through the door of the Puckerbrush Café balancing the car seat in one hand and toting a diaper bag on the other shoulder.

"It's great to see you too, Martha." Abigail laughed as she placed Archer and the car seat down on the closest table.

"Oh stop. You know I'm always happy to see you." Martha put her arms around Abigail and gave her a hug.

"I know." Abigail said as she began to unbuckle Archer. "I guess I'm getting used to this sweet baby being in greater demand than me." She picked him up from his car seat, kissed him on the cheek and passed him off to Martha.

68

"You're getting so big." Martha pulled him close hugging him tightly. "What are you feeding this kid? He's growing like a weed."

"We've been giving him formula every other feeding because he's got an appetite just like his father's." Abigail laughed. "I can't keep up with him."

"That means Grandma Martha will be able to keep him soon." Martha grinned as Archer made a cooing sound. "I think he likes that idea."

Abigail spotted Emily and John sitting at the table across the room. "Those two look in deep conversation."

"Emily had a scare yesterday." Martha said as she bounced Archer on her hip.

"Really? What kind of scare? Is she all right?" Abigail asked.

"She's pretty shaken up. She went to her mother's house yesterday and there was someone in the house when she opened the front door." Martha explained. "She called the police and they got him out."

"Him? Who was it and what was he doing there?" Abigail smiled at Archer as she waited for Martha to answer.

"It was her father."

"You're kidding. I thought he was long gone." Abigail's mouth gaped open in surprise.

"So did Emily. I'm not sure about the whole story, but I guess he told the police he owned the house. John has a lawyer looking into all the legal stuff for Emily. I hope they can get it all worked out." Martha shook her head.

"Me too. That had to be a huge surprise." Abigail glanced over at the couple who were deep in conversation.

"I think it was. It seems she's confused and I completely understand why. I mean he just walked out on her and her mother and now he shows up out of the blue and makes himself at home in his dead wife's house. I guess he wasn't alone. He had a guest. It seems pretty fishy to me." Martha pretended to hold her nose.

"A guest? Poor Emily." Abigail sighed. "I mean everything she has gone through with her mother and now this. I hope she knows if she needs anything, she has all of us."

"I'm sure she does, but just in case, you could go over and tell her." Martha tipped her head in Emily's direction. "I'm sure it would do her good to hear it again."

"I'll do that," Abigail replied.

"Archer and I'll be right here having a conversation. You just take your time." Martha made a baby noise as she smiled at Archer.

"Try not to enjoy yourself too much." Abigail laughed as she walked toward the table where Emily and John were sitting.

"I hope I'm not interrupting. I just wanted to say hello." Abigail put her hands on the back of their chairs.

"You're not interrupting at all." John stood and gave Abigail a hug. Emily followed right behind him. "Are you here for lunch?"

"Actually, Archer and I just stopped by to see Matthew and I couldn't be this close and not stop in here to see you guys."

"Martha would've never forgiven you." Emily attempted a smile as she pointed in Martha's direction.

"You're right about that." John laughed.

"I could tell something was wrong. Martha told me what happened yesterday. I hope you're all right. I know it had to be a surprise." Abigail put her hand on Emily's arm.

"It was." Emily looked away.

71

"If you need anything at all, you just have to ask. Matthew and I will help you any way we can." Abigail offered. "Matthew knows some of the officers around there. He could have them watch the house for you. All you have to do is say the word."

Emily put her hand on top of Abigail's. "I do know that. I'll be fine, but it helps knowing I have all of you guys here for support. John and I've been talking it through. We have to wait and see what the lawyer says. I know I didn't do everything I should have to keep him away."

"Don't be so hard on yourself. You were taking care of your mother and yourself and you did a great job. There aren't a lot of people who would've been able to handle what you did. I can understand how your father would be the last thing you'd worry about." Abigail noticed Emily's eyes glancing in Martha and Archer's direction. "Why don't you go see Archer. I'm sure he would love a hug from his Auntie Em."

"Auntie Em. I like that." Emily smiled as she quickly disappeared in Archer's direction.

"Are you sure she's doing all right?" Abigail asked John as they both watched Emily take Archer from Martha. "I mean that had to be a big shock for her to find her father in her house."

"It was a huge shock and the fact he had someone with him." John shook his head. "She says she's all right, but I'm not so sure. When the lawyer gets back to us, she might feel a little safer. Right now, she's angry he thinks her mother's things are his." John smiled as he watched Emily talk to Archer.

"I know how much you love Emily. You hold on tight to her and make sure she feels loved and safe. That will help her get past a lot of angry feelings." Abigail looked directly at John so he understood what she was saying.

"I will. I promise."

Abigail sensed his sincerity. She and Matthew both knew how much having someone who loved and supported you meant. "She'll be fine then."

73

CHAPTER EIGHT

"Thanks for coming." Matthew greeted Emily and John as they walked through the front door of the Puckerbrush sheriff's office, shaking John's hand and giving Emily a quick hug. "Let's go in my office."

Emily walked through the doorway of Matthew's office and noticed Piper, in uniform, leaning against the credenza behind Matthew's desk, his arms folded across the front of his chest. "Piper. What are you doing here?"

"What a greeting." Piper laughed. "It's nice to see you too, Emily."

"You know I didn't mean it that way. It's always good to see you." Emily gave him a hug and stepped out of the way so John could shake his hand. She was always amazed how close the three of them had become since they found out they were related. It seemed so easy. The resemblance was unmistakable between her, Piper, and Matthew, with their dark hair and dark eyes.

"We didn't know you were in Puckerbrush, Piper. Normally you stop by the café and have a piece of Mom's apple pie before you do anything else." John waited for Piper's answer.

"This isn't a normal visit." Piper's tight smile showed he was serious.

"I don't like the sound of that." Emily took turns looking at Matthew and Piper. "What's going on?"

"Take a seat, both of you." Matthew pointed to the chairs in front of his desk as he moved around the back and sat down in his chair.

Emily took John's hand and held on tight. She sensed some tension in the air and it was making her uncomfortable.

"I asked Piper to come here and help me share some information we learned about your mother." Matthew cleared his throat.

"Information? What kind of information?" Emily squeezed John's hand a little tighter.

"We got reports back from the coroner on the cause of your mother's death. Piper and I asked if we could be the ones to pass it along to you." Matthew paused. "It seems she was poisoned."

"What!" Emily exclaimed. She glanced between Matthew and Piper, trying to process what she heard. "You can't be serious. I mean I didn't think she was sick enough to just pass away, but with Alzheimer's patients, you never know."

"That's why an autopsy was performed," Piper said. "They want to rule out foul play when a death is unexpected. You mentioned at her last checkup your mother was in good health except for her Alzheimer's."

Emily nodded but couldn't say anything. She kept looking at Matthew and Piper waiting for them to tell her this was a joke. They were always joking around with her, quickly making her part of the group, but this was not funny at all. Neither of them said anything. They were looking at her as if they were waiting for her to speak.

"What happens now?" John asked, finally breaking the silence in the room.

"It seems the poison was put in what she ate that night for dinner." Matthew explained. "Susie Chandler, your mother's nurse that night, told the doctors you'd brought her a cinnamon roll and she made sure it was served to your mother with her dinner that night. Other than your cinnamon roll, she was served the same food as the other patients."

"Yes, John and I went to visit her to give her one of the cinnamon rolls we'd made. It was her recipe we used and I wanted her to have one." Emily tried to keep her voice from cracking. Her mother remembering how they would make them together meant everything. It was the closest her mother had come to remembering her in a long time.

"You understand we have to ask you these questions?" Matthew assured her in a sympathetic voice.

Emily nodded as she attempted to process what Matthew was saying. It was so much to take in.

"Piper's the sheriff in Johnson County, where your mother lived. He should be the one talking to you, but I asked him if he would come here and we could do it together because we care about you." Matthew explained.

"Wait, you guys can't possibly think Emily would do anything like poison her mother?" John asked.

"We want to find out what happened," Piper replied. "To be able to do that, we have to rule out everything and everyone. Even Emily."

"Come on, Piper." John sat up in his chair, snapping at his friend. "You can't possibly think Emily had anything to do with poisoning her mother. She and my mother made those cinnamon rolls. We all ate one. Mom, me, Emily, Charles, and even you Matthew." John pointed at Matthew across the desk.

"They were really good." Matthew smiled as he rubbed the back of his neck.

"They were so good, we put them on the menu at the café." John explained. "There's no way..." John paused. "Maybe you should look into why Emily's father suddenly showed up out of nowhere instead of blaming her for something you both know she wouldn't do."

Piper held up one hand. "We're looking into Emily's father. When we find him, we'll get his story, but what we need to know right now is every step you took from the time you made the rolls until you left the roll with your mother."

"I can tell you exactly what we did." John glanced at Emily.

"If it's all right, we'd rather hear it from Emily." Piper pointed to Emily.

"All right." Emily sat back in her chair, closed her eyes as she paused and thought back to that day. "I found the recipe when I was unpacking some boxes. I asked Martha if she would help me make them. She gathered all the ingredients and placed them on the table in the Puckerbrush Café kitchen. I mixed them and rolled out the dough. Martha mixed the cinnamon and sugar and melted the butter. We put them together. I took them home to let them rise."

"Why did you take them home?" Matthew asked.

"I wanted them to be a surprise for John. I couldn't leave them in the café kitchen for him to find." Emily looked at John and smiled. "He's always doing something nice for me. I wanted to do something nice for him."

John leaned over and kissed her.

"Where was John when you made these rolls?" Piper asked.

"I was asleep in the back room. I started cooking early that morning. It was after the noon rush so I went and took a short nap."

"What next?" Piper looked at Emily.

"I got up the next morning and baked them in the oven at home, let them cool, iced them and then took them with me to the café so we could have one for breakfast," Emily looked at John for his confirmation of her recount of the day.

"When did you take one to your mother?" Matthew asked.

"That day. I asked John if he would go with me to take her one. Martha put one of the rolls in a container. It was never opened until my mother opened it to smell the roll." Emily again looked toward John waiting for him to agree with what she remembered.

"She's right. We left from the café and went directly to see her mother." John nodded.

"There wasn't any time in there you were alone with the container?" Matthew asked.

"No!" Emily exclaimed. "It was sitting between us in the car all the way. I carried it into my mother's room, gave it to her, she fell asleep, I covered her with a blanket, kissed her, and left. She was holding the roll when we left her room."

"You both left together?" Piper asked.

"Of course." Emily explained. "We drove there together, so of course we left together."

"You weren't out of each other's sight the entire time you were there visiting your mother? To go to the bathroom or anything like that?" Piper pointed back and forth between the two of them.

"We walked in together, we visited my mother together, we left together." Beginning to panic, Emily moved up to the edge of her chair. "Why do you keep asking?"

"Susie told one of the officers she seemed to remember John leaving the room before you," Piper said.

"Why would she say that? I don't remember even seeing Susie when we were there." Emily looked at John. "Not at all."

"Susie was nowhere around when we were there that day." John put his arm around Emily's shoulder. "Why would Susie lie to you about that?"

"I don't know." Matthew leaned back in his chair. "I guess Piper and I need to find that out."

CHAPTER NINE

"I can't believe either Piper or Matthew would think I would do anything to hurt my mother." Emily threw herself down on the couch in their living room, watching as the sun's reflection coming through the window made designs on the living room ceiling. John sat down next to her and pulled her close.

"You know they had to ask you those questions. They were just doing their jobs."

Emily curled up against John. "I know, but it doesn't make it hurt any less."

"I'm sure it doesn't. Maybe it would hurt less if you put yourself in their place. I'm sure it wasn't easy for them to ask." John kissed her forehead. "You know those two guys care about you, they're family and would do anything to protect you."

"I know." She whispered. "I'm so glad you brought up my father. He didn't even enter my thoughts when they told us my mother was poisoned. I guess I'm still giving him credit when I shouldn't be."

"I'm sure they'll find him and question him."

"I hope so." Emily sighed.

"Sometimes it's hard for me to believe it's only been a few short years you've been in our lives. I've known Piper and Matthew forever, but then you walked into our lives...my life and blew me away." John smiled.

Emily leaned her head back and looked at the smile on his face. "I did?"

"Yes, you did." John sighed. "I'll never forget the day I saw you in the Puckerbrush Café. You were sitting at the table talking with Matthew and Abigail. You looked like an angel and..."

"You thought I looked like an angel?" Emily interrupted.

"I could almost swear I saw a halo above your head."

She placed her hand against John's chest and pushed lightly. "You're lying now."

"No, I'm not. It might have been the sun shining in the window behind you now that I think about it." John grinned.

"I'll buy that. The halo thing, not so much." She laid her head back down on his shoulder. "There has certainly been a lot happening in these past few years. Did I tell you Cathy from the TV morning show called me?"

"No, you didn't. What did she want? Another interview?"

"Yes, but a different subject. She wanted to talk to me about my mother and her disease. She's doing a special on Alzheimer's and she asked if I would talk about being a caregiver to someone with Alzheimer's. Maybe do a fundraiser in my mother's name for Alzheimer's Association."

"That sounds like a great idea and what a tribute to your mother. Are you going to do it?" John asked.

"I've been thinking about it. We talked before my mother..." Emily paused for a second. "passed away."

"I'll be right there with you if you decide to do it. I think it would be a good way to pay tribute to your mother."

"It would be, but not right now. Maybe when I'm ready." She took a breath to keep the tears at bay.

"I can understand that." John agreed. "You know, you may have lost your mother, but think how much our family has grown in Puckerbrush and beyond the past few years. It was just Mom and me until Abigail showed up in Puckerbrush to write her article."

Emily laughed. "I remember you telling me what a big fan of Leeza McBride's books your mother is. I can imagine how excited she was to learn that Abigail was Leeza McBride."

"She was crazy excited." John laughed. "I think the pictures we took with Abigail that day are hanging up on the wall of fame in the Puckerbrush Café."

"I've never heard you call it that," Emily said.

"What? The wall of fame?"

"Yes. I think I've looked at all the pictures hanging on that wall inside the café, but I didn't know that's what it was called." Emily explained.

"I don't remember when we started calling it that, but that's where pictures of everything special that happens in Puckerbrush go. I think Abigail's article is framed and hanging up there, the pictures we took with Leeza McBride are hanging there. I believe the last thing Mom hung on the wall were pictures from our wedding." John explained.

Emily smiled, thinking of the joint ceremony she and John shared with Martha and Charles. "I'm going to have to take a closer look at that wall next time I'm there." Emily took John's hand. "Thank you."

"For what?" John asked.

"For making me forget about what happened today if only for a little while." Emily paused. "I know it was hard for Matthew and Piper to ask me about our last visit to my mother. I just don't understand why Susie would lie about us."

"Me either." John shook his head.

"She's looked after my mother more than anyone else at the care facility. She has always taken excellent care of her and has always been really nice to me. She made sure I knew what kind of day Mother was having or if she thought of something my mother needed."

"That's nice," John said.

"I know." Emily straightened up on the couch. "She would even call me just to tell me something my mother said about me. She wanted me to know the times my mother would remember me. I would write what she told me down in a notebook so I could read it when I needed. It doesn't make sense that she would lie about us leaving at different times."

"We have to trust Matthew and Piper will do their jobs and find out the reason. You know they're going to do everything they can to get to the bottom of this mystery." John pulled her closer.

"I know they will. It's really hard. I wake up some days and think I'll go visit her today. I think maybe it will be a good day for her and she'll remember me." Emily paused. "Then I remember she's gone."

"I know how hard this has to be on you. Matthew and Piper are doing their part to help. I'm here to help you through this. You know my mother, Abigail, and Berta are there if you ever need to talk. You're not alone. I know they can't take the place of your mother, but they love you just the same." John kissed her forehead.

"That means so much to me. You're right about what you said before, our family has grown beyond Puckerbrush." Emily snuggled closer to John as she realized for the first time in a long time she didn't feel alone. There were so many people who cared about her. She felt safe, protected, and loved and Puckerbrush was where it all started.

CHAPTER TEN

"Thanks for coming here to meet with me." Samuel Piper took a seat behind his desk after closing the door to his office.

Emily sat down in the chair in front of Piper's desk, placing her purse on the floor next to her. "I didn't mind. It gave me a chance to get out of the office. I haven't been getting much work done lately anyway." She didn't understand why she was so nervous. It was Piper, not a stranger. "When you called, it sounded important."

"It is." Piper pulled his chair closer to the desk and opened a folder in front of him. "We've found out what happened to your mother. I wanted you to be the first to know before we made a public statement."

"You found out who poisoned her? Who?" She straightened up in her chair. "What happened? Was it my father?"

"My deputies spent a lot of time interviewing everyone who works at the facility where your mother was living and looking into your father. They checked and double-checked everyone's alibis." Piper rubbed the back of his neck. "I'll get right to the point. Susie Chandler has been arrested for poisoning your mother."

"Susie?" Emily stopped talking and breathing long enough to let Piper's words penetrate her thoughts. There were so many questions, so many thoughts, so many pictures of Susie running through her mind.

"One of my deputies became suspicious when he was interviewing Susie and the other employees so he started digging into Susie's past. It seems she's worked at a few different care facilities over the years and had another patient in her care die of mysterious circumstances."

"Susie?" Emily finally took a breath. "Did the care facilities know this? Why did they let her work there? Don't they do a background check on their employees?" Emily kept firing questions at Piper as her thoughts went through all the interactions she had with Susie. There was nothing she could remember that would've made her think Susie was capable of doing something so evil.

90

"I don't understand. Susie was good with my mother. She took care of her every need. She was always there when I visited letting me know how my mother was doing, if she was having a good day or a bad day. She seemed to be on top of everything when it came to my mother. In fact, there were nights she stayed late doing something from my mother." Emily ran her hand through her hair.

"The care facility explained Susie came with excellent references. As far as the other patient who died in her care, there was no conclusive evidence."

Piper's eyes looking directly at her let Emily know he was trying to help her understand.

"I can see why you would be confused about all this. Let me tell you what we found out and it might make a difference." Piper took a piece of paper out of the folder in front of him. "I'll get right to the reason why Susie said she did what she did. It seems she was in love with your father."

"What!" Emily exclaimed. "My father?" She thought back to the day she found her father in her mother's house. She remembered finding the two dirty glasses and plates while she was picking up. She also remembered her mother's bed looking as if there had been two people sleeping there. Anger began working its way through her body replacing the disbelief. "I knew he had something to do with this. What else?"

"From what my deputy could get out of Susie, she and your father have been seeing each other for a while now. They met when your father would come to visit your mother."

"What do you mean?" Emily interrupted Piper. "My father never visited my mother." She waited for Piper to explain for what seemed an eternity.

"From what Susie told my deputy, your father stopped by now and then in the past few years." Piper sat back in his chair. "She told my deputy she always made sure he could get in the facility and visit. According to Susie, he was trying to get a sense of how far your mother's Alzheimer prognosis had progressed. I understand your mother and father were still legally married." Piper waited for her answer.

"Yes, they were." Emily stopped and took a breath. "You see, when my father left my mother, she was unable to understand what was going on. She didn't even realize he was gone. She was in no shape to sign divorce papers. My father knew they would never hold up in court."

"From what my deputy gathered from Susie is that your father was waiting for your mother to pass because he knew he would still inherit her estate." Piper leaned forward in his chair.

"Susie also wanted your father to be free to marry her. She decided the only way that would happen was if she took things into her own hands and your mother was no longer in the picture."

Emily watched as Piper didn't look up from the piece of paper.

"Susie told my deputy your father didn't know anything about what she planned. She thought the night you brought your mother the cinnamon roll would be a good night to carry out her plan because she could try to place the blame of your mother's poisoning on you. Then she and your father would be free to marry."

She caught Piper's gaze as he finally looked up from the piece of paper he was holding. From the expression on his face she could tell this was as hard for him to tell her as is it was for her to hear. Her body tensed as anger rushed through her body again replacing any feeling of confusion that had snuck in before. She couldn't speak. All she could do was try to control the thoughts of betrayal from Susie and her father. The man who betrayed her before, had done it again.

"Are you all right, Emily?" Piper asked.

"I don't know." She finally answered as Piper's words registered. "I don't know."

"This has to be difficult for you to hear, but I wanted to be the one who told you. I didn't want you to hear this from anyone else but me." Piper stood and walked around to the front of his desk, taking a seat on the corner.

"I know how much your life has changed in the past year and I wanted you to know that I'll always be there for you and I know Matthew, Abigail, Martha and especially John feel the same."

"Thank you, Piper. That means a lot to me." Emily managed a half smile. "Right now, I don't know how I feel."

"I know this is a lot for you to take in. I thought maybe you could stick around for a little while. We could talk, maybe go to lunch. It would give me a good excuse to get out of here for a while." Piper smiled.

"Thanks, Piper." Emily reached up and touched his arm. "I appreciate all you're doing, have done, and will do. I know you're trying to help." She stood from her chair. "I think right now what I need is to be alone. I need to try and sort through all you've told me and I can do that better alone."

"If you're sure." Piper stood. "I don't think you should really be alone right now. Maybe just have lunch with me."

"I'm sure. I'm fine." Emily gave him a hug. "What I want to do right now is get back to Puckerbrush and see my husband. I can use the time while I'm driving back to sort through everything you told me so I'll be able to answer all the questions John's going to ask." She paused and looked at Piper. "Where's Susie now?"

"My deputy booked her into the county jail. She'll be seeing a judge sometime today."

"Will she be let out on bail?" Emily asked.

"That'll be up to the judge. I've instructed my deputies to make sure the judge knows that from what we found out about her past, she's a flight risk and she needs to stay locked up. I think with her background the judge will deny her bail." Piper explained.

"Good," She turned to walk out Piper's office doorway.

"Will you call or text me when you get back to Puckerbrush? I'd like to hear from you and make sure you're all right." Piper placed his hand on her back as he walked with her through the lobby.

"I will."

Piper opened the front door for Emily to walk out. "Be careful driving home. Make sure you tell everyone hello for me."

Emily nodded as she walked out the door and took in a breath of fresh air. She was glad she came alone. She needed time alone and driving back to Puckerbrush would give her that time to gather her thoughts. To try and put in place all that happened, everything Piper told her.

"Make sure you call or text me when you get back to Puckerbrush," Piper repeated his request.

"I will." She turned around and took one last look at Piper. "I promise."

She needed time. Time to try and decide how she was going to process what she'd learned and how it was going to change the way she dealt with other people. To find a way for this not to affect the way she treated everyone in her life she felt she could trust. How many times do you allow one person to do something to change your life forever? She wasn't going to let her father bring her to her knees again. He'd done that to her once when he walked out on her and her mother. She picked herself up that time and learned to take care of herself and her mother. He wasn't going to destroy her life again. She wouldn't let him.

CHAPTER ELEVEN

"I was wondering if we could talk?"

Emily stood with her hand gripping the doorknob, glaring at her father standing in the doorway as she tried to fight the urge to slam the door in his face. "How did you find me?"

"I stopped at the Puckerbrush Café and talked to John. I convinced him to let me know how to find you." Henry Clayton said.

"I'm going to have a talk with him when he gets home." She replied through clenched teeth. "I don't have anything to say to you."

"Don't blame John. I told him I had some signed papers to give you. Just give me five minutes." Henry Clayton held his hand up to stop the door as Emily began to shut it. "I'll stand right here. I won't even come in. All I want is to tell you how sorry I am for everything. Everything beginning the day I walked out on you and your mother."

"If that's all you want, then forget it. I don't accept your apology and I never will." Emily tried to close the door all the way without success. "You need to leave."

Henry stood in place, his hand against the door and his gaze locked with hers. "I'm good with you not accepting my apology, but I would really like you to know that I had no idea Susie was planning to harm Dorothy in any way."

"Don't!" Emily exclaimed as she held her hand in the air. "Don't you dare speak her name. You lost that right the day you packed your bags and walked out on her."

Henry stopped and stepped back as he looked at Emily. "She was my wife as well as your mother, Emily. I loved your mother. I still love her."

Gripping the doorknob tighter as anger filled her body, she raised her voice. "Oh, I see. That's how love works as you see it. She was worthy of you as long as she was well and could take care of you. When she failed to do that, you couldn't do the same for her. When she needed you, it was all right for you to walk out on her and not even care if or how she was taken care of. Now you expect me to believe you when you say you loved her?"

"I didn't mean it that way." Henry looked down at the ground. "I really didn't mean it that way. I didn't know how to take care of her and I was scared, but that doesn't mean I didn't love her."

"You don't think I was scared?" Emily put her hands on her chest. She could feel her heart racing. She took a deep breath to try to calm herself. "I was nineteen years old. I didn't know how to take care of her either, but *I* learned. She needed you and you didn't have enough courage to stick around and make sure she was taken care of. You were so scared all you could do was walk out on a woman who you promised to love and cherish in sickness and in health. You walked out on your own wife and left your daughter to take care of her."

She looked her father up and down as she waited for him to reply. He said nothing. "Your five minutes are almost up." Emily broke the silence.

"I realize you may never forgive me for walking out on you and your mother. I can live with that. What I couldn't live with is the idea you believe I would do anything to physically harm your mother. All I want you to know is I had no idea Susie was going to harm her. If I had, I would have stopped her. I would have never let anyone hurt Dorothy." Henry eyes locked with Emily's again.

"You're the only one who could do that. Right?" Emily pretended to check the time on her watch. "You're five minutes are up. You need to leave now." Emily held a finger in the air. "Before you do, tell me why..." Emily paused and took a breath. "Why you showed up and tried to claim this house and my mother's estate?"

Henry looked downward.

"You can't tell me why? You show up after all these years and think you have a right to anything my mother has." She waited as he never looked her in the eyes.

"I'm broke." Henry moved his foot back and forth in front of him, pretending to brush something away. "I thought if I showed up, you'd forgive me."

102

"Really? You thought I would be so happy you came back I would forgive you for all the pain and heartache you caused then share everything my mother had left with you?" Emily laughed. "You are so wrong."

Henry Clayton slowly turned and began to walk back to his car. Emily watched as he walked out of her life again. This time was completely different than it was the first time. The first time she ran after him begging him to stay. She told him how much she loved him and needed him in her life. She begged him to stay and help her take care of her mother. She remembered him not even looking back. He kept walking. She watched him believing he would turn around and come back. He never did.

This time she could care less. She couldn't feel anything expect pity for him. Pity for all the things he missed out on and would miss out on. When she and John had children, they would never know who he was. As far as she was concerned, her father was dead.

****

Emily didn't look up when John walked through the front door. She continued to stare at the same blank space on the wall she'd been staring at for the past few hours. She'd been playing over and over in her mind the conversation with her father and the memories of the first time he left her and her mother.

"I'm home." John bent down and gave her a kiss before he sat in the chair next to her. "Is everything all right?"

"My father stopped by to visit." The tone of her voice must have let him know she wasn't happy. "Why did you tell him how to find me?"

"He said he had signed papers to give you. He promised he wouldn't stay long." John explained. "I texted you to let you know."

"No, you didn't!" Emily exclaimed.

John glanced at his phone. "Crap! I forgot to hit send. I'm so sorry you were surprised. Did he have papers? Is that what happened?"

"No, it wasn't."

"Tell me what happened. I would've never told him how to find you if I'd known he was going to say something to hurt you."

"Oh, he told me he was sorry. He also wanted to let me know he still loved my mother and if he had known Susie was going to harm her, he would have done something about it." Emily laughed. "He actually wanted me to believe he had nothing to do with my mother's death."

"I can tell you don't believe him," John said.

Emily finally moved her gaze from the blank space on the wall to look directly at John. "My father killed my mother the day he walked out on her. He'll never be able to convince me he would've stopped Susie from hurting her. He'll never be able to convince me he cared about her at all. If he cared about her like he said, he would've never walked out on her. He would've stayed and taken care of her or done whatever it took to make sure she had the care she deserved. He might as well have been the person who poisoned her."

"I'm really sorry, Emily." John took her hand in his. "I didn't mean to do anything to upset you. I thought he would give you papers and leave."

She squeezed his hand. "I understand. If I never see him again, it'll be perfectly fine with me. As far as I'm concerned, my father died the day he walked out on my mother and I. From now on, I plan to keep it that way." Emily looked at John. "I also found out he's broke. That's the reason he showed back up. He thought I would forgive him and share everything my mother had left with him."

"I hope you set him straight."

"I did. He's gone for good now."

Emily again locked her gaze on the blank space on the wall. She began to run through her conversation with her father and the memories she'd tucked away years ago. This time they were disappearing as fast as they appeared, never to be thought of again.

CHAPTER TWELVE

"Should we wait until Piper gets here to order?" Abigail glanced at Matthew who was sitting next to her at their favorite table in the Puckerbrush Cafe. "Archer's asleep and I didn't have a chance to eat lunch. I'm starving."

"Why don't we go ahead then. Piper should be here any minute." Matthew turned around to see if Martha was around. "I'll go up and order us each a bacon cheeseburger. How does that sound?"

Abigail smiled as he stood up from the table. "That sounds wonderful."

Matthew leaned down and gave her a kiss. "Anything for you."

"I knew there was a reason I married you. You like bacon cheeseburgers almost as much as I do." She laughed as Archer made a few noises from his car seat.

"I better go get it ordered. I don't know how long he's going to be asleep."

Matthew disappeared to the counter as Abigail turned to look out the window. It seemed so long ago when she first sat down at this table. It was the day she came to Puckerbrush. It was the first time she met Matthew. She looked down and smiled as Archer made faces in his sleep. "I've got a lot to be thankful for and you're one of them." Abigail touched his little feet as he pulled them closer to his body.

"You look deep in thought." Matthew sat back down next to her.

"I was thinking back to the first time I got to take in this view of Puckerbrush." Abigail waved her hand in front of the window. "It seems so long ago, but it was only a few years. How things have changed."

Matthew took her hand. "I remember that day. It was the day you and I met for the first time. Things have certainly changed since then. All for the good. By the way, I ordered your cheeseburger."

She let out a huge sigh. "Thank you. I'm so hungry."

"Hi you two." Piper interrupted as he walked up to their table shaking Matthew's hand then leaning down to give Abigail a quick peck on the cheek. "How's my Archer?" He sat down in the chair next to where Abigail placed Archer's car seat. "Man, he's getting big."

"He's growing up so fast." Abigail smiled.

"Yes, he is." Piper took Archer's hand which disappeared in his. "He seems happy to be here."

"As long as he's fed and his diaper is dry, he's a pretty happy boy." Matthew laughed.

"I think we all would be happy in that situation." Piper smiled. "I know I am."

"You guys are hilarious." Martha said as she set Abigail's cheeseburger down on the table in front of her. "Here you go."

"God bless you, Martha." Abigail picked up a fry from her plate and took a bite. "I'm so hungry."

"Matthew, you need to make sure this one eats now and then." Martha placed Matthew's burger on the table in front of him.

"I'm trying. Things can get a little hectic at our house now that Archer's here," Matthew replied.

"You just tell me when and I'll make you something to take home with you. Anytime." Martha glanced at Piper. "What can I get for you?"

109

"It's good to see you too, Martha." Piper smiled.

"You know I'm always happy to see you, Piper." Martha made her way around the table and gave him a hug. "Now, what do you want to order? I don't want people just loitering around in here."

"I want the same thing they're having. It looks really good." Piper held a finger up in the air. "Of course, I'll have a piece of apple pie also."

"Make that two." Matthew chimed in.

"Three." Abigail looked at both of them and smiled.

"Coming right up." Martha laughed as she disappeared behind the counter.

"What did you want to meet with us about?" Matthew asked before he took a huge bite of his burger.

"I thought I would let you guys know I did that interview with a reporter for one of the papers in Houston."

"So. How did the interview go? I remember them wanting to talk with you." Abigail interrupted.

"Pretty good. I think." Piper leaned back in his chair. "I don't know if we're getting anywhere with all this."

"What about the genealogist? Have you or your father heard anything?" Matthew asked.

"Not yet. It shouldn't be too much longer." Piper crossed his arms in front of his body. "I believe my father said they would have everything finished soon. It was going to take several months to research since we didn't have much information to give them as far as Edward Dalton was concerned."

"I think we gave them everything we had after the first of the year. Right?" Matthew asked.

"I gave them everything I could find." Abigail took a bite of a fry. "I made a rough family tree, if that's what you want to call it, filling in all the information I had on you two and Emily."

"I would just like to make sure we find everyone out there that might be even the least little bit related to us. I wouldn't be surprised if someone walked through the door any day like Emily did."

"Did I hear my name being spoken?" Emily's voice came from behind the group. She walked up as all of them laughed and greeted her.

"You have a way of just walking in at the most opportune times." Abigail stood and gave her a hug. "It's good to see you."

"You two. And of course, it's nice to see these guys also." Emily gave Matthew and Piper a quick hug then took an empty seat at the end of the table.

"I stopped in to pick something up for lunch. John promised me a chef salad." Emily smiled in Archer's direction. "How's our baby?"

"He's doing fine. It must be nice to have someone prepare lunch for you and all you have to do is pick it up." Abigail glanced in Matthew's direction.

Matthew put his hands up in the air. "You heard Martha. All you have to do is let her know and she'll make you something."

"Boy, I heard what she said completely different than you did." Abigail laughed. "Besides, Emily doesn't have to pack up a baby in order to go anywhere."

"I think she's got you on that point." Piper chimed in.

"Don't put me in the middle of any disagreement." Martha handed Piper his cheeseburger across the table. "I learned a long time ago not to take sides."

"Can I get you a burger also?" Martha asked Emily.

"No. John promised me a chef salad. I just came in to pick it up. I've got some research I'm in the middle of so I have to get back." Emily explained.

"You want me to go get it for you?" Martha pointed toward the kitchen.

"No, thank you though. I think I'll go make out with my husband for a few minutes before I go back to work." Emily jumped up from the table and jogged across the room.

"She's certainly doing better after all that happened." Matthew kept his voice down so Emily didn't hear him.

"I think she's dealing pretty well. I know John said it was hard for her at first." Martha sighed. "She didn't want to talk about it at all then finally she opened up."

"That's great," Piper said. "I'm glad she has John and you to talk to. I hate that Matthew and I were the ones who had to put her through it."

"I know what you mean." Matthew nodded his head.

"She doesn't blame you guys at all. She loves you two. You both tried to help her in your own way. She knows that." Martha sat down in the chair Emily left empty.

"I hope she knows we're not going to abandon her like her father did." Piper ate one of his fries.

"You two big lugs have hearts of gold and it shows when you deal with anyone." Martha reached and took one of each of their hands. "Emily knows you guys are always going to be there for her. There's nothing going to change that. If she wasn't making out with her husband, I'm sure she would tell you herself."

"Speaking of making out." Abigail changed the subject. "You said you were going to stop and see Regina. When are we going to get together with you two, Piper?"

"Making out made you think of Reggie?" Piper looking down at his plate and moved around his fries.

"We've been talking about us getting together. I thought I would ask how she was and see if you guys talked about it." Abigail glanced at the baby. "Archer has an appointment with her in a few weeks. I can ask her about it then."

"She's a godsend to Puckerbrush. I've only heard good things from everyone in town," Martha said.

"I'd tell her what you said, Martha..." Piper paused. "and I'd ask her about getting together with you and Matthew, Abigail, but Reggie and I aren't seeing each other anymore."

"What!" Martha exclaimed.

"What happened?" Abigail asked.

114

"I think we remembered why we broke up in high school. Reggie's very determined and always has been. She wants to make a go of her practice here in Puckerbrush. It was hard for us to find time to spend together. Her being here in Puckerbrush and me being in Johnson County."

"I'm sorry, Piper." Matthew interrupted.

"It's fine. Really. Reggie and I are much better off as friends instead of a couple."

Piper's phone ringing saved him from the awkward moment. "Samuel Piper." He answered. "All right. Of course." Listening to the voice on the other end of the line, Piper finally spoke. "They're right here with me. I'll talk to them and get back to you with a date and time." He paused for another second. "Of course. I'll call you back as soon as I can." Piper ended the call.

"What was that about?" Matthew asked.

Piper took a second before he answered as if he was gathering his thoughts. "That was Cathy."

"Cathy the producer of the CBS AM Show?" Abigail asked.

"Yes." Piper paused for a minute. "She said someone called her asking for information about us. She said it was a woman who would like to meet with us. She wanted to know when we could all meet with her. She's willing to come to Puckerbrush since we are all around here."

"Did Cathy tell you anything about her?" Matthew asked.

"Only that she believes she has some information for us." Piper shrugged.

"I'd say we grab Emily before she leaves so we can find a date and time we can all meet with her." Abigail glanced at Matthew then at Piper who were both nodding in agreement.

CHAPTER THIRTEEN

"He's pulling up right now." Abigail stood at the window of the Puckerbrush Café as she held the bottle Archer was happily drinking from. "It looks like he's waiting for the people in another car that's pulling in next to him."

"I can take Archer and feed him while you guys talk." Martha offered.

"If you don't mind. It would probably be better." Abigail carefully handed Archer off to Martha without the nipple of the bottle ever leaving his mouth.

"I don't mind taking care of this little guy at all." Martha talked baby talk to Archer all the way to the kitchen.

"Don't be feeding him any apple pie," Matthew called after Martha. "Save that for me."

Martha ignored him as she walked through the kitchen doors.

"I think I've been replaced." Matthew pouted.

"No one is ever going to replace you in Martha's eyes. You know that." Abigail gave him a hug.

"Martha said Piper's here." Emily walked out of the kitchen doors into the dining room.

"He's coming in now." Abigail pointed to the front door of the café.

"Abigail, Matthew, Emily, I'd like you to meet Heidi Collins and her son, Peter."

Piper walked in the dining room followed by a beautiful woman, dressed sharply in tailored slacks and blouse. Abigail guessed she was in her mid to late forties. A man who looked to be around the same age as Piper, Emily, and Matthew, walked in behind her. Abigail stopped breathing for a second when she got a closer look at the man. His dark hair and eyes were almost an exact match for both Piper and Matthew. He was even around the same height. If a stranger walked through the door and was asked, they would say Matthew, Piper, and now Peter were related until they got to know Matthew and Piper. Peter seemed different in his actions. He seemed uninterested in being there. Abigail watched as he inspected the Puckerbrush Café with a look of disdain. Unlike Heidi, Peter wasn't smiling.

118

Matthew walked up and shook their hands. "I'm Matthew Thompson and this is my wife, Abigail." Matthew motioned for Abigail and Emily to join them.

Finally gathering her thoughts, Abigail walked up to greet the two, Emily following behind. "It's nice to meet you." She couldn't seem to take her eyes off Peter. "I can't get over how much you look like Matthew and Piper. I can even see a resemblance to Emily." Abigail turned to Emily.

"I see what you mean. It's uncanny." Emily laughed.

"Why don't you come sit down." Matthew pointed to a larger table in the middle of the room. "Piper told us you had some information for us."

"Piper?" Heidi Collins looked confused.

"They call me by my last name Piper."

"I see." Heidi nodded. "I like that." She took a seat at the table. Peter sat down next to her brushing off the chair first. "I think we might have some information for you. I see you noticed the resemblance between Peter, Matthew, Emily, and Samuel." Heidi glanced at each of them as they took a seat at the table.

"It's striking how much they look alike." Abigail agreed. "May I ask how old you are, Peter?"

"Thirty," Peter said. His expression not changing.

"Around the same age as Matthew, Emily, and Piper, I mean Samuel." Abigail corrected herself.

"Let me start at the beginning." Heidi sat up in her chair placing her elbows on the table. "I got pregnant when I was a teenager. I went to the father and he said it wasn't his child and didn't want anything to do with Peter."

"I'm sorry. That must have been hard." Abigail interrupted.

"My mother's one of the strongest women I know." Peter spoke up. "She's put up with a lot of negative talk from people in town. I've listened to it all my life."

"Everything turned out to be for the best except Peter doesn't know his biological father." Heidi glanced at Peter with an expression of adoration most mothers show their children. "Peter was raised by a wonderful man and our lives have been good. I wouldn't change anything. Anyway, I saw Samuel in an interview on the morning show I watch. I couldn't get past how much he looks like my Peter and also the man who's Peter's biological father."

"When my mother showed me pictures of you, it was like looking in a mirror." Peter pointed to Matthew, Emily, and Piper.

"Who is Peter's biological father? Do you mind if I ask?" Piper waited for her reply.

"Not at all. His name is Joseph Wright." Heidi paused.

"Joseph Wright? Where do I know that name from?" Piper looked around the table to see if anyone was thinking the same.

"It does sound familiar." Matthew agreed.

"Probably because he's the preacher at the big mega church outside of Dallas," Heidi replied.

"You mean the mega church that's on TV every Sunday morning?" Matthew raised his eyebrows.

"That's the one." Heidi pointed a finger at Matthew showing him he was correct. "The Wright Way Church. I knew Joseph before the church was a mega church. My family belonged to the church when I was younger and Joseph's father, Martin, was the preacher. I haven't been back since Joseph lied about being Peter's father."

"Can I ask what happened when you told him?" Abigail waited for Heidi's answer.

"I confronted him and of course, he denied it." Heidi leaned forward in her chair and waved her hand in front of her. "I even went as far as finding a lawyer to prove it. I don't know how, but he managed to prove by DNA he wasn't the father. After that, I gave up. My family couldn't afford to do much more and I didn't know what else I could do. I eventually got married and my husband loves Peter like he's his own." Heidi smiled as she took Peter's hand in hers.

"If his DNA didn't match Peter's, I don't know what we can do to help you." Piper rubbed the back of his neck. "I mean, I agree Peter looks a lot like all of us, but that doesn't prove anything."

"I don't know how Joseph did it, but I know somehow he falsified the DNA test. I'd never been with a man before Joseph. There was no way Peter could be anyone else's child. When I first met Joseph, he was the youth pastor at the church. He was very kind and sweet, full of charm. I was young and naïve and believed he loved me." Heidi looked down at her hands in her lap.

Abigail watched closely as Peter put his arm around her to comfort her. It wasn't natural. It seemed a forced show of comfort. It was as if he was the adult and Heidi was the child.

"Joseph and his family have a lot of money and I'm sure they could buy the results they wanted. I didn't have the money to fight them." Heidi twisted in her chair. "When I saw Samuel on television and realized how much he looked like Peter then heard his story, I thought maybe it was a path worth examining. I know it's a long shot, but it's one I'm willing to take."

"What do you know about Joseph Wright's past?" Abigail asked.

"Unfortunately, most of what I know that made me contact you is secondhand information." Heidi wrung her hands in front of her. "I do know his family because, like I said before, my family belonged to their church. His father, Martin Wright, was the preacher when my family started attending the church. Joseph took over for him when Martin started preparing to retire. Joseph's mother is a wonderful woman, but she's so quiet." Heidi frowned at the thought. "I always thought she was shy, but after getting to know her better I came to realize she was a woman who felt her opinion wasn't important and had probably been told that all her life. It's very sad."

"I'm confused. What exactly is it you want us to do?" Matthew asked.

Heidi sat up in her chair and looked directly at Matthew, but before she could speak Peter stopped her. "I would like to test my DNA against yours to see if there's a connection." He placed his hand on top of his mother's as if to let her know he would take it from here.

"I know this is a long shot, but you see my mother told me there were always stories going around that Joseph Wright was not the biological child of Martin Wright. There was talk about Martin and another man who started the church together when they were younger. Rumors say Joseph was the biological child of Martin's partner who disappeared one summer. The mother of the child gave Joseph to Martin to raise because she couldn't."

"That's right." Heidi pulled her hand out from under Peter's and looked directly at him. "When I heard Samuel's story of the traveling evangelist, I knew I needed to find all of you because Martin Wright's partner who disappeared would hold traveling tent revivals."

"You think Martin's partner was Edward Dalton?" Piper asked. "I'm sure there was more than one traveling evangelist around at that time."

Matthew glanced in Abigail's direction.

"You have to admit there is more than one coincidence; the traveling revival, the fact Peter looks a lot like all of you. I mean I would like to find out if there is a connection." Heidi replied. "If he is, that could mean Joseph is Edward Dalton's son. Which would also mean I might be able to prove, once and for all that Joseph is Peter's father. I would like to put to rest what I tried to prove so many years ago. Also, I would like for Peter to get what he deserves from Joseph Wright." The tone of Heidi's voice went from calm to determined.

"And what's that?" Abigail asked as she tried to understand the change in Heidi's personality.

"For Joseph Wright to admit he's Peter's biological father. I know it's been hard for Peter to know his own biological father wouldn't admit he was his child."

"That's all you want?" Abigail tilted her head as she noticed Heidi begin to tear up.

"That would be enough for me." Heidi took a deep breath and sat back in her chair.

"What about you, Peter? What is it that you want?" Abigail waited for his reply.

"I want the truth to come out and my mother to be proven right, and finally put all the lies to rest." Peter looked as his mother instead of anyone else at the table. "I would also like the world to finally know what kind of man Joseph Wright is."

Something about his answer bothered Abigail but before she could dig further, Emily spoke. "It would be easy enough for me take a sample and do a DNA test." Emily glanced around the table. "I am a scientist. I have access to the testing equipment," she explained to Heidi and Peter.

"I'd be more than happy to pay for any expenses." Heidi offered.

"If it does come back that Peter is related to us, that would mean we found another cousin named Joseph Wright." Piper glanced at Matthew and Abigail.

"I don't know of any reason why we shouldn't do a test." Matthew shrugged.

"If you want to follow me back to my office, I have access to everything we need to get a sample there." Emily stood from the table and waited for Peter and Heidi to do the same.

Abigail watched as they said goodbye to everyone. Either her writer sense of what would be a good plot twist in a story or her normal people sense were telling her something wasn't quite as it should be. When they received the results of Peter's DNA test, she would know for sure if there was any reason she should be concerned.

CHAPTER FOURTEEN

"What now?" Matthew asked as he took a seat on the couch next to Abigail. Archer began to wiggle as he settled down to nurse.

"I guess we need to call Heidi and Peter and let them know the news and welcome Peter to the family of Edward Dalton." Abigail tightened her grip around Archer to try and keep him in place. "It's really their call what they do next with the information we give them."

Matthew wrapped his fingers around one of Archer's feet and smiled. "How could anyone not want anything to do with a child you fathered? I can't imagine not ever seeing Archer. I know he's only a few months old, but it's like I've known him all my life and I can't imagine it without him in it."

"That's what I love about you and what makes you a wonderful father." Abigail leaned over and kissed Matthew's cheek. "Archer is pretty perfect, isn't he?"

"I couldn't ask for more." Matthew smiled. "Well, maybe a little girl someday."

"Someday, maybe." She locked eyes with Matthew. "Maybe next time you can be the one to be pregnant for nine months and then be in labor for over eight hours or longer."

"I would if I could, but I don't think that's going to happen." Matthew laughed. "Let's talk about what to do with the information we found out about Peter."

"Nice way to change the subject." Abigail adjusted Archer a little after he moved around when he heard Matthew's laugh. "What did Emily say when you talked to her? Did she want you or Piper to call Heidi and Peter to let them know?"

"She said she didn't care who broke the news to them. She was going to email the results of the DNA test to Peter tomorrow." Matthew made a cooing noise at Archer. "I think one of us should probably call him and tell him the results before he receives an email surprise."

"I'm sure he's been waiting to hear the results. It's been a few weeks since Emily did the test." Abigail's questioning expression must have been obvious to Matthew.

"What are you thinking?" Matthew asked.

"I wish I felt good with how this is going to work out." She sighed.

"Are you worried about something?"

"I told you the day we met with Heidi and Peter I didn't think Peter was telling us the truth about what he planned to do with the information if it turned out he was related to all of you." Abigail tilted her head sideways. "If Joseph Wright doesn't admit it or submit another DNA sample, there's no way Peter can prove he's his father. He can only prove he's related to you, Emily, and Piper."

"I remember you voicing your concern, but it's out of our hands. It's up to Peter and Heidi what they do with the information we give them. It'll be a long road for them, and you're right, all they can prove is that Peter's related to Emily, Piper, and me. We don't have any direct DNA proof that we're related to Edward Dalton."

"I know." Abigail agreed. "I guess all we can do is give them the information we have and let them do with it what they will. I told you I didn't get a good feeling from Peter. I could be completely wrong though."

"We give him proof that he's related to Emily, Piper, and I. We only have Robert Piper's word that Edward Dalton was his biological father." Matthew shrugged his shoulders. "I mean Eldon didn't even tell you Edward Dalton's name. All he told you was that the traveling evangelist was the father of his daughter's child and my grandfather." Matthew leaned back on the couch. "I know when I first found all this out, it was hard for me to believe. If we hadn't had my grandmother's journals along with Eldon's journals, I don't know if I would be convinced it was true."

"I know. It's a big puzzle and we're missing a few key pieces. We have a lot of circumstantial evidence but no real proof." Abigail paused. "I don't see how the information we give Peter is going to help him prove he's the actual son of Joseph Wright who he believes is the son of Edward Dalton."

"I think that's out of our hands also. All we can do is tell him what we know. He'll have to decide what he does with that information," Matthew said.

"I know you're right." Abigail nodded. "Hopefully, whatever they do with it, it'll be for the best. Both Heidi and Peter said they only wanted to prove that Peter was Joseph Wright's son. We'll give them the information and wish them luck."

"Now that's settled, I'm going to go to work. I'll call Peter from there. What if I take Martha up on her offer and pick something up from the café and bring it home for dinner tonight?" Matthew asked.

"That would be terrific. How about some of her chicken fried steak? I've been craving that." Abigail pleaded.

"You got it. Maybe I'll even add a slice of apple pie." Matthew ran his finger up Abigail's arm.

"You're the best husband ever." Abigail leaned over and kissed him.

"I know." Matthew laughed. "I'll let you know how it goes with Peter. I know he'll be happy to hear the news." Matthew stood and waved as he walked out the door.

"I wish Eldon was here to help us through this." Abigail looked at Archer who had fallen asleep in her arms. "Eldon would know exactly what to do."

****

"Hi Peter. It's Matthew Thompson."

"Matthew. I've been waiting for your call. I'm assuming your calling because you have news," Peter said.

"I do." Matthew leaned back in his office chair. "I guess I should say welcome to the family. It's a dysfunctional family, but we manage."

"Thank you, Matthew. I don't seem to remember any dysfunction when I met all of you. You were all what I expected."

Matthew was surprised by the lack of emotion or humor in Peter's voice. Maybe he wasn't in a joking mood today. "You probably didn't hang out with us long enough. Anyway, Emily should be emailing you all your test results. That should give you any information you need about the tests she did. Other than that, I don't think we can help you any further to prove you're related to Edward Dalton except our word."

"I appreciate all you've done so far. I feel like with proving that I am related to you, Emily, and Samuel, I'm one step closer than we were before."

Matthew was surprised by Peter's answer. "One step closer to what exactly?"

"I know I have a long way to go to prove Joseph Wright is my biological father. I do feel like I'm getting closer." Peter paused. "I just need that one missing piece, or should I say person, to be able to link all of this together. When we find that, we'll be able to move forward with our plan."

Matthew suddenly understood what Abigail meant by getting the feeling Peter wasn't being totally honest with them.

"You know we aren't giving up looking for any more people who might be out there. Now that you're one of us, we'll make sure and keep you in the loop." Matthew leaned forward in his chair and placed his elbows on his desk in front of him.

"Thank you again for calling, Matthew. I'll be sure and fill my mother in on everything and I'll watch for Emily's email."

"We'll talk soon." Matthew barely got out the words before Peter ended the call. He rubbed the back of his neck as he leaned back in his chair again. Peter was one determined man. Like a dog with a bone, he wasn't going to give up until he found that missing piece.

CHAPTER FIFTEEN

"Piper, there's someone here that would like to talk to you. Do you have a minute?" A deputy stood at Piper's office doorway.

"Sure. I'll be right out." Piper checked the calendar on his phone thinking he might have missed an appointment. There was nothing. Since he and Reggie decided to stop seeing each other, his calendar was empty. Walking out of his office into the lobby he spotted a sharply dressed older woman seated in the waiting area, her legs crossed and her purse lying neatly across her lap as she clutched it with her hands. Sitting next to her was a younger woman who shared her same features, the same eyes and high cheek bones. The older woman's dark hair had greyed but must have been the same color as the younger woman's, at one time. Her beauty had been passed down.

"I'm Samuel Piper. I understand you would like to talk to me." The older woman stood extending her hand for Piper to shake. She couldn't seem to take her eyes off him. He was more intrigued with the younger woman's smile.

"Yes." The woman nodded. "My name is Penelope Johnson-Harris. This is my granddaughter Lydia."

Piper returned her smile with a nod.

"If you have a few minutes, I would like to talk to you about Edward Dalton."

Piper's eyes widened as he couldn't find words. Not only was he taken back by Lydia's beauty but hearing Edward Dalton's name spoken by a complete stranger also took him by surprise. "Of course. Why don't we go in my office where we'll have a little more privacy?" Piper motioned toward his office door.

"We don't want to take you away from anything important. After all, I don't have an appointment. I knew I should have called first to let you know we were coming, but this is something I needed to do in person."

"It's perfectly fine," Piper said.

"I thought if we drove here, I wouldn't be able to back out. If I called, I could have hung up the phone." Penelope walked through the office door and took a seat in one of the chairs in front of Piper's desk followed by Lydia.

"Lydia took time away from her job and insisted she come with me." Penelope touched her granddaughter's knee and smiled. "It's a good thing we enjoy each other's company."

"It's perfectly fine. You didn't take me away from anything that can't wait." Piper sat down in his chair. "I apologize, but you took me by surprise when you mentioned Edward Dalton's name."

"I could tell. It's been a long time since I've spoken his name." Penelope looked down at her lap as she adjusted herself in her chair. "Lydia did some research for me on social media since I'm not very good at that type of thing. I do good to work the remote to the television." Penelope winked at Lydia. "Anyway, the San Angelo television station where you did your interview on the morning show gave us your name. It's taken me a little while to get up the nerve to contact you. Like I said before, I was going to call, but this is something I needed to do in person."

"You have me interested. Thank you, Lydia for helping your grandmother find me." Piper smiled at Lydia. "And making sure she arrived here safely."

"You're welcome." Lydia eyes lit up as she returned Piper's smile.

"Lydia's a nurse at Baylor University Hospital. We're all very proud of her." Penelope looked in her direction. "She works way too much which means she doesn't have much of a social life. Her taking the day off is my way of getting her out and about and having some time alone with her."

"I have the same problem. Maybe I need your suggestions on how to change that." Piper glanced at Lydia and smiled then returned his attention back to Penelope. "Now, what exactly did you want to tell me about Edward Dalton."

"Edward Dalton was the father of my first child."

Piper knew the surprise on his face registered with Penelope. He needed a second for the words she spoke to sink in. He could tell by her reaction this was as difficult for her to talk about as it was surprising for him to hear. She couldn't look directly at him. She looked down at the floor as she continued. Lydia reached across the arm of the chair and took her hand.

"We were young and I was so infatuated with Edward." Penelope touched her face with her hand. "We spent a lot of time together when we were younger. We were always together at church functions and Sunday afternoons. I felt I could trust him. He always made me feel special especially that night. He told me God had brought us together for a reason. I tried to stop him."

Piper watched as Penelope opened her purse and took out a Kleenex and wiped her eyes.

"Anyway, I found out I was pregnant a few weeks before Edward disappeared. When I told him, he said it must be God's plan and promised we would talk about it when he returned from his revival trip. He never returned." Penelope paused. "I'm sorry. I didn't think I would get emotional about this after all these years. Like I told you, I haven't spoken his name in a long time."

"It's all right, Grandmother. We knew this was going to be hard for you to talk about." Lydia patted her hand.

"You and Edward Dalton have a child together?" Piper asked as he noticed the deep concern for Penelope in Lydia's eyes.

"Yes. A son." Penelope finally looked up, tilted her head and took a minute to look directly at Piper. "I don't mean to stare, but my son looks a lot like you."

"You know what he looks like? Then you must know where he is." Piper waited for Penelope's reply.

"Yes, and his name is Joseph." A smile crossed her lips and then disappeared. "I gave him up as a baby. I was so young and I didn't have a way to provide for a child on my own. My family told me they couldn't and wouldn't help me if I kept him."

"That must have been difficult for you." The hurt in her expression was obvious to Piper. Lydia did her best to comfort her by holding on to her hand.

"Yes. It was." Penelope wiped her eyes.

"Do you know where Edward went for his revival trip?" Piper asked.

"He would always go out on revival during the spring and summer months. I believe this trip was somewhere in Texas. Small towns around this area. Let me try and explain." Penelope sat up in her chair. "Edward and his friend, Martin Wright, started a small church together when they were young men. Martin always stayed behind and took care of the church while Edward would travel and do revivals across the state during the spring and summer months. This time when Edward left, he never returned."

Goose bumps covered Piper's body.

"I'd made up my mind before I gave birth to the baby I was going to give it up. He was a beautiful baby. The way he came into this world wasn't his fault." Penelope wiped her eyes again as memories overtook her. "I wrapped him in a tattered blanket and took him to the church. I left him with Martin Wright hoping and praying Martin would find a good home for my son. He deserved that much."

"And did he?" Piper asked.

"Yes. I learned quite by chance years later that Martin and his wife took my son and raised him as their own. No one ever knew the baby belonged to Edward and I, not even the baby."

"You said his name's Joseph. How do you know that? Where is your son?" Piper asked.

Penelope took a few seconds to answer. "The church Martin and Edward started became a mega church. I believe mostly because of Joseph. Perhaps you've seen it on television on Sunday mornings. Joseph grew up as part of that church. That's how I knew what happened to him."

"You saw him on television?" Piper asked.

"I did," Penelope replied.

"And you knew Joseph was your son?" Piper asked.

"Yes. Joseph has an unmistakable resemblance to Edward. Again, Lydia did some research for me and it seems Joseph took over the church for Martin several years ago when he retired and has made a name for himself as a preacher."

"Does he know who you are?" Piper asked.

"No." Penelope shook her head.

"You sound pretty sure about that."

Penelope's expression turned serious. "I am." Penelope put her hand on her chest. "Martin promised me he wouldn't tell anyone, including Joseph, about me. And I've never reached out to him."

"What about Edward?" Piper put his elbows on his desk as he leaned forward. "Do you think they told him about Edward Dalton being his biological father?"

"I'm not sure whether or not they've told him about Edward being his father. I've never heard anything about or from Edward since he left that spring. I moved away from the Dallas area shortly after the baby was born. I couldn't be in the same town as my son. It was too hard. I met my husband, married, started a new life and tried to forget. I was blessed with a wonderful family." Penelope glanced over at Lydia and smiled.

Piper agreed with Penelope as he studied Lydia. She was beautiful. He was having a difficult time keeping his mind on their conversation and not locking his gaze on her. "Does your family know about Joseph?"

"Now they do. My Johnny knew before we married. I wouldn't marry him without him knowing and I couldn't come talk to you without telling my family first." Penelope explained.

"Grandmother called everyone together for a family meeting a few weeks ago when my parents were here for a visit," Lydia replied. "She told us all then. She explained how she saw you on television and realized she couldn't stay quiet."

"I'm sure it had to be hard for you to tell them." Piper could see this was another painful part of their conversation by the expression on Penelope's face. "Exactly why did you feel you needed to come talk to me?"

"I felt maybe I could help you. Something painful from my past could do some good. I remember you saying in your interview that you'd connected with the other two people..."

"Mathew and Emily?" Piper interrupted.

"Yes. I remember you saying they found each other through DNA testing. I'm sorry I can't give you a DNA sample for my son or for Edward, but I can tell you where Joseph is. I thought maybe if you had that information, there might be a way for you to find a connection." Penelope paused. "I know it's a long shot, but at least now you know there's a person out there who has the same DNA as Edward Dalton."

"So, his name is Joseph Wright?" Piper asked.

"Joseph Wright. Yes. He's the preacher of the Wright Way Church in Dallas." Penelope pulled her phone out of her purse and handed it to Lydia. "Will you find that picture, please."

"Oh course, Grandmother." Lydia took the phone and began searching.

As Piper watched, he thought back to the conversation he, Matthew, Emily, and Abigail had with Heidi Collins and her son Peter. He'd heard of Joseph Wright before that meeting, but would have never in a million years connected him with Edward Dalton until now. He didn't want to mention Peter to Penelope, not until he was sure.

Lydia held up her cell phone showing Piper a picture. "This is Joseph."

Piper studied the picture on the phone. That was Joseph Wright. The well-groomed man with the charismatic smile was the same person he Googled after the meeting with Heidi and Peter. He was Penelope and Edward Dalton's son. This was his, Matthew, and Emily's uncle. The connection Joseph had to everyone in his family began running through Piper's mind.

"Unfortunately, I don't have anything to give you in the way of proof of what I'm saying. I'll do whatever you need me to if it will help you with your search. I know in my heart I did the best thing for my son by giving him up." Penelope attempted a smile. "He's had a good life with Martin Wright. A much better life than I could have given him." Penelope cleared her throat. "I see Edward in him." Penelope looked at the picture Lydia searched for then placed her phone back in her purse.

"Oh, there's one more thing I have for you." Penelope pulled an envelope out of her purse and handed it to Piper.

"What's this?" Piper turned the envelope over and inspected it.

"I jotted down all the names I could remember from Edward's family. I did my best to remember everyone I could. It's been a long time."

Piper pulled the folded piece of paper from the envelope and began reading the names.

"This is great. We didn't have any names of Edward's family members. In fact, my father hired a genealogist to find what he could about Edward's family. This will help his research. Thank you."

"I wish I could do more," Penelope replied.

"You've done a lot. I'd like to get your information so we can contact you if that would be all right." Piper pushed a notepad and pen across his desk. "I want to talk to Matthew and Emily to see what they want to do with this information." Piper watched Penelope write her phone number and address on the piece of paper.

"I'll have Lydia write down her phone number just in case you can't reach me." Penelope pushed the paper in front of Lydia and smiled.

"I'd be happy to." Lydia began writing. "Like Grandmother said, please call me if you need to."

"I really appreciate you coming to me and telling me your story. I know it couldn't have been easy for you. I remember how difficult it was for my father to tell me my grandmother's story. He'd promised her he would take it to his grave." Piper thought back to the day he found his father sitting at the kitchen table waiting for him.

"I thought I would never have to talk about this either." Penelope reached across the desk and took Piper's hand. "I know how hard it was for your father. He must love you a lot to share his story with you when he made a promise to his mother. I guess God had different plans."

"Thank you. Joseph and my father would be half-brothers." Piper stood from his chair.

Penelope nodded. "That would be right."

"I'll be in contact with you, Ms. Harris."

Penelope smiled and stood from her chair. "Call me Penelope. After all, I feel like we have a connection."

"Penelope it is." Piper put his hand on her back and walked her out of his office into the lobby, Lydia by her side. "Have a safe trip home." He watched as they walked out the door. He couldn't help but think how many people were touched by Edward Dalton's legacy. The circle kept getting bigger and Penelope Johnson-Harris handed them a glimpse into Edward Dalton's past they didn't have before.

CHAPTER SIXTEEN

Picking up his cell phone, Piper searched for Matthew's number and selected dial. "Hey Matthew."

"Piper. What's up?"

"I just had an interesting meeting." Piper leaned back in his desk chair. "I met with a woman named Penelope Johnson-Harris and her granddaughter Lydia. She happens to be the mother of one of Edward Dalton's children." Piper waited for what he knew was coming.

"You're kidding me." Matthew exclaimed.

"No, I'm not," Piper said after he received the reaction from Matthew he waited for. "She came to see me today. Cathy from the Am San Angelo show shared my information with her. The three of us had a long talk and Penelope left me some information."

"You mean on Edward Dalton?" Matthew asked.

"Yeah. She left me a list of names of some of Edward's family members. At least the names she could remember." Piper ran his finger over Lydia's name written on the pad of paper, remembering her beautiful smile.

"That's great."

Piper sensed the excitement in Matthew's voice. He couldn't wait to tell him the rest of Penelope's story. "There's also something else I need to tell you."

"You mean it gets better than this?"

"It seems the child Penelope Johnson-Harris and Edward Dalton are the parents of is none other than Joseph Wright." Piper waited again for what he told Matthew to sink in and the name to register.

"You mean the Joseph Wright who Heidi and Peter told us about. The preacher at the mega church?"

"That's the one." Piper smiled.

"Wait." Matthew paused. "That means Peter would be Penelope's grandson. If we can prove he's Penelope's grandson, then we would be closer to proving Peter is Joseph's biological son which is what Heidi and Peter wanted."

"You got it." Piper let out a laugh. "I made sure I got her address and phone number before she left."

"Good. Oh man. I can't wait to tell Abigail about this." Matthew's voice was filled with excitement. "There's something I want to share with you that Abigail told me."

"What's that?" Piper asked.

"You know Abigail has good people sense."

"Yes, I do. She's been right on about everyone she's met," Piper replied.

"I know. It's a little eerie, but anyway, she told me she got a strange feeling that Peter's not being honest with us about what he wants out of this situation."

"You mean about what he wants from Joseph Wright?" Piper asked.

"Exactly. I'm not sure what to make of it, but I trust her. Maybe we should be careful with how we approach Peter and Heidi with this news."

Piper took a second to think about what Piper said. "I agree with you. Maybe you, me, and Abigail need to get together and decide how we're going to go about sharing this information with Heidi and Peter."

"Let me tell Abigail what you found out and then we'll call you and we can discuss our next steps. How does that sound?" Matthew asked. "Oh course, we need to talk to Emily and get her opinion. Why don't you call her and I'll talk to Abigail then we'll get together?"

"It sounds good to me. I'll wait to hear from you guys."

"Great. We'll talk soon Piper. Thanks again for letting me know what you found out. I think we might have found our missing piece of the puzzle."

Piper ended the call, leaned forward and picked up the envelope Penelope Johnson-Harris left him. "I hope you're right, Matthew."

****

"You're kidding me?" Abigail sat up on the couch watching Matthew's expression trying to tell if he was joking.

"I'm not. Piper called me this afternoon. I guess this woman, Penelope Johnson-Harris and her granddaughter Lydia, got his information from Cathy at the AM San Angelo Show. They just showed up out of the blue." Matthew sat down next to Abigail on their couch.

"I wish I could've been there to talk to them myself. I would've loved to have met them. There are so many questions running through my head right now." Abigail placed her hand on her forehead.

"I know what you mean. When he was telling me this, I couldn't believe it."

"What do you think we should do? Do you think we could meet them? Did you tell Emily? Do you think they would talk to the four of us? I would love to know more about Penelope. There's so much I want to ask her about Edward Dalton." Abigail couldn't get the questions out fast enough. "Does she know Edward is dead?"

"Take a breath." Matthew put his hand on Abigail's arm. "You're going to run out of air if you keep going."

"I am not!" Abigail exclaimed.

"Piper got her address and phone number before they left. He's calling Emily to tell her what he knows. I'm sure we can call Penelope and talk to her or maybe even set up a time we can all go and meet with her."

"That would be so great. I have a good feeling about this. She just might be the missing piece we need to put all of this mystery together." Abigail clapped her hand together. "Let's call her."

"I told Piper I would talk to you and then we would call him and talk about what we all wanted to do." Matthew paused. "I also told him about the feeling you got about Peter."

"You did? What did he say?" Abigail asked.

"He trusts your feelings like I do. I told him we need to all decide together what we want to do with this information and how we want to proceed."

155

"I agree." Abigail sighed.

"I know we may not move as fast as you want to, but if we all agree on how we're going to go forward, what we're going to tell Heidi and Peter and when, it'll be easier for all of us," Matthew explained.

"And because I don't believe Peter's being honest with us about what he wants from Joseph Wright, I think we should go slow and make sure we protect Penelope. After all, she felt it was important enough to tell Piper. I'm sure that took a lot of courage." Abigail thought back to how long Eldon kept his secret. She and Matthew were the only ones who knew Eldon had killed Edward Dalton and buried his body. If he hadn't killed Edward, what would have happened to Penelope? These were thoughts she decided to keep to herself. No good would come from revealing the secret Eldon had trusted her with.

CHAPTER SEVENTEEN

"Come in, come in." Penelope Johnson-Harris stepped back and motioned for Matthew, Piper, Emily, and Abigail to step inside the doorway into the living room. "I can't believe how much you two men look like Edward Dalton." She stood back and inspected Matthew and Piper. "You must be Emily because you resemble these two handsome men. So that leaves Abigail." She extended her hand for Abigail to take.

"It's a pleasure to meet you." Abigail smiled. "I'm not sure what to call you Ms. Johnson-Harris or Ms. Harris."

"Just call me Penelope. That'll be perfectly fine."

"Penelope it is." Abigail nodded. She looked exactly like she thought she would. From the description Piper gave her, the picture in her mind was very close. She reminded her a little of Martha, who was currently caring for Archer.

Penelope was a more petite woman who put extra effort into her appearance, not one hair was out of place. It was pulled back neatly in a bun. Grey had overtaken her black hair from when she was younger. She was a beautiful woman who Abigail imagined any man would have been drawn to.

"I'm Matthew Thompson. Abigail's husband." Matthew shook Penelope's hand. "This is Emily and you remember Samuel Piper."

"Of course, I do. Samuel, Lydia, and I had a nice talk in his office. My Lydia was quite taken with Samuel." Penelope smiled in Piper's direction. "I understand you're also a sheriff, Matthew."

"I am. In Puckerbrush which isn't far from Piper."

"Piper?" Penelope gave Matthew a questioning look.

"I'm sorry. Samuel." Matthew corrected himself. "We all call him Piper."

"You look like a Piper." Penelope smiled as she glanced at him. "But Samuel is so much more distinguished."

"Did you hear that Matthew. Samuel is much more distinguished. Maybe you should change what you call me." Piper put his hand on Matthew's shoulder.

"I've only known you as Piper. I know it would be too hard for me to change now."

"I'm so happy to have all of you here. I feel like I know each of you from watching Samuel on television. I enjoyed his story of how all of you connected, especially you Emily. Such an interesting story to tell. Let me get you something to drink. I have tea and coffee." Penelope offered.

"I'm good for right now." Abigail glanced at Matthew, Emily, and Piper who all nodded in agreement.

"Then come sit down." Penelope made her way to a straight-back chair next to the couch and waited for everyone else to settle. Abigail, Matthew, and Piper took a seat on the floral-patterned couch and Emily sat in the twin straight-back chair at the other end.

"I'm sorry my granddaughter, Lydia, couldn't be here today. She was scheduled to work and couldn't get the time off. She would've loved to have been here to see you again, Samuel."

"I would've liked that." Piper sat down at the end of the couch trying to avoid the looks the others were giving him.

Penelope saved him from any explanation. "I'm so happy all of you came here so we could meet. I'm not sure what more I can tell you. I told Samuel everything I know about Edward Dalton. I even gave him a list of the names I could remember. It was so long ago." Penelope sighed. "My memory isn't what it used to be."

"We appreciate everything you've done. Especially telling your story to Samuel," Abigail said. "We've had a difficult time finding anything about Edward Dalton. We thought..." Abigail glanced at everyone. "I thought it would be good if we could all come talk to you. Get to know you. I hope that's all right?"

"Of course, it's perfectly fine." Penelope patted Abigail's knee. "I'm glad to help in any way I can. I'm just not sure what else I can tell you."

"It's not so much what you can tell us, Penelope." Piper interrupted. "What we're wondering is if we could ask you to give us a DNA sample."

"I don't understand." Penelope took turns looking between Piper, Emily, Matthew, and Abigail. "Why me?"

"We believe Joseph Wright, your son, might have fathered a son, Peter Collins." Emily could see the confusion in Penelope's expression.

160

"When Lydia did some research on Joseph, there was nothing about him having children. Why would you need my DNA?" Penelope placed her hand on her chest.

"Peter Collins is a son by a woman who found herself in a similar situation as you did with Edward only with Joseph." Emily tried to explain as she watched Penelope tear up.

Matthew tried to eliminate some of Penelope's confusion. "Peter and his mother, Heidi, came to us and asked us to help them prove Peter is who he says he is. We thought if we could prove he's your grandson, then we would be closer to helping them prove he's Joseph's son."

"How will my DNA sample help you prove this Peter Collins is Joseph's son without his DNA? No one knows Joseph is my son except Martin and his wife." Penelope wiped a tear away.

"Thanks to my father, we already know Peter has Edward Dalton's DNA. With yours, we would be able to prove that Peter's your grandson—yours and Edward Dalton's." Piper attempted to explain.

Abigail moved closer to the edge of the couch and Penelope. "We know it's a longshot, but we thought if we could prove Peter is the grandson of you and Edward Dalton, they could maybe go to Joseph with this information." Abigail searched Penelope's face for any clue she might be reluctant.

"I can't believe this." Penelope put her hands up to her cheek. "Joseph turned out to be like his father. I hoped and prayed he didn't inherit any of his father's horrible genes." Penelope's eyes opened wide as she looked at Abigail. "So, you're going to confront Joseph with this information about Peter?"

"Peter would like to. He wants to know whether or not Joseph is his father." Abigail straightened her posture and softened her tone. "When I first came to Puckerbrush, I was only going to write an article for a friend's magazine and then go back to my life in Chicago." Abigail smiled at Matthew.

"Then I met Matthew and so many other people who changed my life. One of those people was Eldon, a man who'd lived in Puckerbrush all his life. You see, he was abandoned as a small child and grew up in the orphanage in Puckerbrush. His daughter became pregnant by Edward Dalton, just like you. She died after giving birth to a son. Her mother also died giving birth to her. Eldon raised his daughter by himself. He had no one to help him raise a grandchild, so he gave the baby to the orphanage." Abigail paused as she watched Penelope's expression change from one of questions to one of sympathy.

"What happened to the baby boy?" Penelope asked.

"He was my father," Matthew replied. "My grandparents couldn't have children so they were happy to adopt my father. He learned he was adopted after they'd both passed."

"That must have been a shock for your father." Penelope said.

"It was, for all of us," Matthew replied.

"We're telling you this, Penelope, because we want you to understand how everyone's life has changed because of and in spite of Edward Dalton." Piper placed his elbows on his knees as he leaned forward in his seat.

"When you and Lydia came to talk to me, I felt like we found one of the missing pieces of the puzzle we're all trying to put together. All of our lives have changed lately. Matthew and I've been friends since we met at the Academy. We had no idea we were related until several months ago."

Matthew interrupted. "But now that we know, we are closer, if that's possible. I always thought of Piper...Samuel, as a brother and then we found Emily."

"What you're trying to tell me is that for every bad thing that has happened because of Edward Dalton, there's been good come out of it." Penelope smiled.

"That's right." Abigail took Penelope's hand. "I know we're asking a lot of you and what we're asking you to do will bring up many memories you may not want to process again."

"But if I do what you want, then maybe something good will come of it. Like Matthew, Emily, and Samuel." Penelope waved her hand in front of her.

"Emily came to us out of the blue a lot like you did, Penelope. She found Matthew when she was searching for her mother's family. Her mother was a child of Edward Dalton's." Abigail explained.

"And how is your mother doing with all of this new information, Emily? It must be a lot for her to process all the new people in her life." Penelope asked.

"My mother passed away a few months ago." Emily looked down.

"I'm so sorry." Penelope placed her hands against her mouth.

"Thank you. She didn't know anything about Edward Dalton. You see she was adopted as a baby and then was diagnosed with Alzheimer's in her forties. I began searching for medical history and that's when I found Matthew." Emily glanced at Matthew and smiled.

"Our family has grown so much in the past year. I can't even tell you how happy we all are to have found each other." Abigail touched Penelope's arm. "We would like to make sure we've found as many people whose lives have been touched by Edward Dalton as possible. If we can put all the pieces together, we'll feel like we've defeated all the wrong he has done."

Abigail looked at Penelope and smiled. She hoped she could see she was telling her the truth and if they could give Peter and Heidi the information they needed to prove Joseph Wright was Peter's biological father, then that would be another wrong they'd overcome.

"What would you like me to do?" Penelope Johnson-Harris asked.

Emily stood up from her chair and reached for the bag she'd placed in the floor beside it. "That's where I come in."

CHAPTER EIGHTEEN

"I have Penelope's DNA results back." Emily sat down at the table in the Puckerbrush Café joining Abigail, Matthew, Martha, and Piper.

"And...?" Abigail asked as she leaned her elbows on the table in front of her, smiling at Matthew beside her and Piper sitting across the table from Matthew. Archer made cooing sounds from his car seat as Martha leaned down to entertain him.

"Peter Collins is definitely Penelope's grandson." Emily placed the piece of paper in her hands down on the table so everyone could see.

"Which means Penelope's right about her and Edward Dalton. They did have a child and that child had a child who is Peter Collins. The question now is whether Joseph Wright is their son." Abigail locked gazes with Emily.

"Science can't help you there without a sample to test from Joseph Wright." Emily sat back in her chair and folded her arms across her body.

"What we do now is tell Penelope the test results and maybe between all of us we can decide our next step." Matthew suggested.

"I can call Penelope and see if I can stop by and see her." Piper offered.

"Of course, you can." Abigail winked.

"What do you mean by that?" Piper narrowed his eyes at her.

"You mean Penelope and Lydia, don't you?" Still grinning, Abigail caught Piper's blush. "You've worked her name into the conversation a lot lately and you've had only nice things to say about her. She must be really special."

Piper took a breath before he answered. "I wouldn't mind seeing Lydia again. I'm telling you she's very pretty."

"I'm sure you're right. If she looks like Penelope at all, I'm sure she's very pretty. I can't wait until I get to meet her," Abigail said. "Hopefully that won't be long."

"I wouldn't mind meeting her either. Abigail's right about you having a lot of nice things to say about her." Martha took her attention away from Archer to join in the conversation.

"I need to find out more about her. I only got a chance to spend a little bit of time with her when she and Penelope were in my office. I did get her cell phone number though." Piper held up his cell and twisted it in the air.

"How did you manage that? I mean she was only there for a short time." Matthew asked.

"I'm learning a lot about you Piper. You must have some charm in there somewhere." Emily smiled as she gave him a wink.

"I have a lot of charm you've never seen before." Piper smiled. "I only pull it out when I want to.

"Well, you do have Edward Dalton's genes," Matthew replied as he sat back in his chair. "From what we've learned about him, we need to be careful when we use those charms."

"Wow!" Piper exclaimed. "I never thought about it that way. I'm a little creeped out right now."

"Me too," Abigail, Matthew, Martha, and Emily said in unison.

"All right! Let's get back to deciding what to do with the information we have." Piper rubbed the back of his neck as he tried to change the conversation.

"I'll let you guys decide this. Archer's asleep so I'm going to go back to the kitchen and finish some cleaning." Martha began walking away. "Let me know if he wakes up or if you need anything."

"We will." Piper waved at Martha. "I'll call Penelope and talk to her. I think what we do from here depends on what she says."

"Matthew told me he let you know how I felt about Peter." Abigail looked at Piper.

"Yes, he did." Piper nodded. "I've learned to trust your instincts about people."

"What did you think Emily?" Abigail asked.

"If you mean about Peter, I didn't get a good feeling about him. When he and Heidi came to my office for me to get a sample from him, I got a strange feeling from him." Emily straightened her posture. "I don't mean scary or anything like that. It was just a feeling that he wasn't telling us the entire truth about what he really wanted out of this. Maybe he has another motive."

"Exactly!" Abigail pointed her finger at Emily. "That's just how I felt when they left here. There was something he wasn't saying. Heidi did a lot of the talking and what Peter did say was what he'd heard or learned from her. It's like he'd been told what to say."

Emily interrupted. "And what he did say was always about him. What he wanted and what he needed. He was concerned about his mother being proven right about his father, but it was more because he wanted it for himself not so much for her."

"That's it, Emily." Abigail interrupted. "It was as if it was all about him. I think they call that a narcissistic personality. I've met people like him before. I was always uncomfortable around them."

"What you guys are saying is that we shouldn't trust Peter?" Piper asked.

Abigail shot Emily a questioning look. Emily nodded. "That's exactly what we're saying."

"All right," Matthew replied. "Do we all agree we are very careful with any information we find out. Peter and Heidi will be told on an as needed basis?"

171

"I think that's the best thing to do. Not only to protect all of us, but to also protect Penelope. She was hurt enough by Edward Dalton in her past. I would hate to see her hurt by Peter." Abigail glanced around the table to make sure everyone agreed before she continued.

"Can you imagine how hard it would be for her to find out for sure her son and grandson both turned out just like Edward Dalton? It's taken her all these years to get past giving up her son. It would break her heart to learn there was another Edward Dalton in the family line."

"You really think he's like Edward?" Matthew asked. "I could maybe see Penelope's son, Joseph, being like Edward, since according to Heidi, he supposedly lied about being Peter's father."

"One of the classic traits of a narcissistic personality is lack of ability to have intimate relationships because they're more important than anyone else. It would mean they would put someone else on the same level or higher than themselves. Other people and their problems are an annoyance to someone like this. Taking responsibility for or caring about someone else besides themselves is out of the question. Narcissists take what they want or need out of a relationship. It's all about them." Emily explained.

"You really think Peter's like that?" Piper asked.

"I do," Abigail replied. "Emily said it perfectly. Peter's in this for himself and what he can get out of Joseph Wright. He's using his mother and her experience of being pregnant with him and Joseph denying it, as a reason to put himself in the spotlight and get what he wants."

"What do you think he wants?" Matthew asked.

"You two are the sheriffs here. You're the ones who are supposed to be able to profile people and determine motive and reason for their crimes. Emily and I are just two civilians." Abigail smiled at Matthew and Piper.

"Well for two civilians, you two sure have a strong opinion about Peter Collins," Piper said.

Abigail winked at Emily. "Yes, we do and who wants to place a wager on whether or not we're right?" She raised her arm in the air as she glanced around the table for takers.

"I'm not touching that bet with a ten-foot pole." Piper held up both his arms in surrender.

"Me either." Matthew laughed.

"Chickens." Abigail smiled.

CHAPTER NINETEEN

"Good morning." Piper waited for Penelope to open the door more than a crack.

"It's so good to see you again, Samuel. Come in." Penelope smiled and waved her hand for him to walk through the door. "Can I get you a cup of coffee?"

"That sounds good. Thank you."

"Just take a seat anywhere. I'll be right back."

Samuel watched Penelope disappear into the kitchen off the dining room. Before he could sit down the front door opened and Lydia walked in. He tried to speak but was caught up in the glow the sun behind her created against her long, dark hair. Her sweater hugged her body, her jeans tucked into her knee-high boots. She was as beautiful as he remembered.

"Hi Samuel." Lydia broke the silence.

"Hello." Piper finally managed to speak a single word.

"Lydia. Good morning." Penelope interrupted as she returned to the living room with a cup of coffee in each hand. She gave Piper one of the cups, handed one to Lydia and then kissed her cheek. "You remember Samuel, don't you?"

"Yes, I do. How are you Samuel?" Lydia asked as she dropped her bag on the couch.

"I'm good. You?" Piper was still having a difficult time concentrating on anything but Lydia.

"Why don't we sit around the dining room table? I'm going to grab another cup of coffee and be right back." Penelope disappeared into the kitchen.

Piper waited for Lydia to take a seat then sat in the chair next to her.

Penelope returned with another cup of coffee in her hands. She pulled out a chair and took a seat. "You said you had some information for me, Samuel. What is it?"

"We received the DNA test results back and they show Peter Collins is your grandson." He watched as Penelope's expression didn't change. The news he just gave her didn't seem to faze her at all. Lydia, on the other hand, did seem surprised by the news.

"You're sure?" Lydia asked.

"Positive." Samuel took a drink of coffee. "We've linked Peter to myself, Emily, and Matthew. We all link back to Edward Dalton, thanks to my father's DNA. Now we can link Peter to Penelope because of the sample Emily took last time we were here."

"It sounds so impossible." Lydia ran her fingers through her hair. "I mean I work in the medical field and I know how the science, but all these people connecting back to one person, Edward Dalton, it is amazing."

Nodding in agreement, Piper said, "I know. I thought the same when we started looking for connections. Now it's seems second nature."

"What do we do now?" Penelope asked.

"That depends on you, Penelope." Piper took another drink of his coffee. "If you want, we can set up a time and place for you to meet Peter and his mother Heidi. It's totally up to you. Emily, Matthew, Abigail, and I feel it's *your* choice. We don't want to put you in an awkward situation. We don't know Peter or Heidi that well and wouldn't feel right telling them about you without your permission."

"What do you think, Grandmother?" Lydia reached across and took Penelope's hand.

"I'm not sure." Penelope locked gazes with Lydia with a sadness in her eyes. "I remember the day I left Joseph with Martin like it was yesterday. It was hard, but I knew it was the right thing to do. I couldn't love him the way a baby deserves to be loved. Would you think less of me if I said I don't wish to meet Peter?"

"No, Grandmother. I could never think less of you for any reason. This is your story and your past." Lydia squeezed her hand. "I know how hard it was for you to share with the family. I can't even imagine how hard it would be to finally see Peter."

Wrapping both of her hands around her coffee cup, Penelope seemed deep in thought. "I have this image of how it would be to meet Joseph and Peter. I would see these handsome, caring men who had grown up in loving homes. Like any mother and grandmother would want for her child and grandchild. I can imagine they have good hearts and pleasant natures and then I would remember Edward." Penelope lowered her gaze and took a breath.

"I know how hard it would be for you to meet them especially after all these years. You don't have to explain anything to me," Lydia said.

"I don't know how I would react if I realized they were anything like Edward. If they'd grown up to manipulate people like Edward did. I wouldn't want to live with knowing that the rest of my life. What I've seen of Joseph on television, which was just a small amount, I didn't really care for. I could see Edward in his actions. If Peter wishes to meet Joseph, I'm fine with it, but I don't wish to be involved." Penelope wiped a tear away.

"I understand completely, Grandmother," Lydia said. "Samuel told us what happens next is up to you. Why don't you think about it for a few days? There's no hurry for you to make a decision."

"Lydia's right, Penelope. You don't have to decide anything right now. Take a few days and if you decide you want to meet him, then we'll set it up. We haven't said anything to Peter or Heidi about you. We want it to be your decision." Piper glanced across at Lydia. The family resemblance was strong, and the concern for her grandmother showed clearly on her face. Was it possible she was even more beautiful than he remembered from the first time they met?

"I think that would be for the best." Lydia smiled at Piper.

"I agree." Piper placed his hands on the table. "I'll fill everyone else in on what we talked about. You can call me anytime if you change your mind. We want to make sure you know everything we do. This situation is something we all take one step at a time."

"That means the world to me. The fact that you, Emily, Matthew and Abigail understand makes me feel better about all this." Penelope smiled at Piper. "Now if I knew Joseph and Peter were as handsome and nice as you, Samuel, I wouldn't hesitate. I had a good feeling about you or I would have never come to talk to you."

"Thank you, Penelope. I feel the same about you. We can thank Edward Dalton for one thing and that's bringing us together." Piper stood. "I have to get back to the office. Remember, you can call me anytime at all." He bent down and gave Penelope a quick hug then turned his gaze to Lydia.

"Why don't I walk you out?" Lydia stood from her chair. "I'll be right back, Grandmother."

"Take your time." Penelope put one finger in the air. "Can you wait just a minute Samuel? I found something the other day and I would like to give it to you." She stood and disappeared into one of the back bedrooms.

Piper glanced at Lydia and smiled as she shrugged and said, "I have no clue."

"Here it is." Penelope returned and handed Piper a black and white photo which dated back many years. "I was going through some old photos and found this one. It's of me and Edward. I think it was taken before he left for his revivals. I would've been pregnant with Joseph then."

Piper could see Penelope's expression change from one of contentment to one of sadness as he took the photo from her hand. "Are you sure you want me to have this?"

"Of course." Penelope attempted a smile. "What on earth would I do with it? It was so long ago and part of a life I would like to forget."

"If you're sure. I know Abigail, Matthew, and Emily would love to see it." Piper glanced at the photo and then at Lydia. "I can't get over how much the two of you look alike. It's like I'm looking at a picture of Lydia."

"There are some strong genes in our family." Penelope smiled at Lydia. "Just like there are strong genes in Edward's family."

"Would it be all right if we passed this along to Peter so he would have a photo of you and his grandfather." Piper looked at Penelope. "We won't give him your information, but I'll leave his information with you. It will be completely up to you if you wish to contact him."

"I guess that would be all right." Penelope paused for a second. "I can't see any harm in letting him have it. After all, it's a part of his past."

"Thank you, Penelope." Piper put the photo in his pocket and took out a piece of paper he'd written Peter's name and phone number on. "Here's Peter's information." He placed it in Penelope's hand and held on. "It's completely up to you if you contact him. We don't want you to do anything you aren't comfortable doing."

"Thank you, Samuel." Penelope squeezed his hand. "You're a sweet man. Your parents should be proud."

"Take care of yourself and we'll talk soon." Piper winked at Penelope then glanced at Lydia. "I'm going to take your granddaughter up on walking me out."

"I'm ready when you are." Lydia started to make her way toward the door.

Waiting for Lydia to walk out the door, Piper followed. "It was nice to see you and your grandmother again."

"It was nice to see you too." Lydia waited on the steps for him to join her. "My grandmother has done nothing but talk about how sweet and handsome you are since she met you. You and Matthew."

"That's nice of her. I've enjoyed meeting her. That's been a good side to all of this. We've gotten to meet some really great people. Edward Dalton may have been a cad, to put it mildly, but everyone his life has touched are really good people, so far." Piper stopped beside his car.

"I was wondering, Samuel..." Lydia paused.

Piper watched as she nervously shifted her feet and looked down. Hopefully she was thinking the same thing he was.

"Would you like to have dinner sometime?"

"I'd like that."

Lydia finally looked at him and smiled. "I'm working the day shift this week if you have any night free."

"It just so happens I do. How about this Thursday?" Piper asked. "There's one condition though?"

Lydia's eyebrows raised. "Condition."

"You have to start calling me Piper. This Samuel stuff makes me feel like I'm back in school and getting in trouble with the teacher." Piper watched as Lydia's smile lit up her face. He could almost swear her eyes sparkled.

"Piper it is. How about seven this Thursday?"

"Seven's good. I'll text you and get your address." Piper opened the door to his car and climbed in. "Tell your grandmother goodbye for me." He started the car and backed out of the driveway keeping his eyes on Lydia who was waving goodbye. "I have you to thank for this Edward Dalton," he murmured to himself.

CHAPTER TWENTY

"I have you guys on speaker phone." Piper placed his phone down in the middle of Abigail and Matthew's dining room table. "Abigail, Matthew, and Emily are here with me in case you two have questions for any of us."

"Good evening everyone," Heidi Collins replied. "Peter and I are here and anxiously awaiting any news you might have for us."

"We do have some news, in fact." Piper glanced at everyone else at the table.

"That's good. What is it?" Peter's tone told everyone he wasn't in the mood to socialize. He sounded anxious to get to the point of the call.

"I'll let Emily share with you." Piper nodded at Emily for her to pick up the conversation.

"Hello Heidi and Peter. It's Emily. I emailed you the test results and also printed them and overnighted them to you along with a photo Penelope wanted you to have, Peter. Did you receive everything?" Emily asked.

"Yes, we did. Thank you so much for the photo. It was a nice surprise being able to see what Peter's grandparents looked like," Heidi said.

"I'm glad you got everything. What you have is proof Peter's definitely related to Edward Dalton and Penelope Johnson-Harris, who according to her, Joseph Wright is her and Edward Dalton's son." Emily paused. "So that would mean, Peter, you are their grandson and the son of Joseph Wright."

There was a moment of silence over the phone. Emily shrugged, looking at the others, not quite sure what to say or do now.

"Are you two still there? Heidi. Peter." Matthew asked.

"Yes. I'm sorry. We're both still here." Heidi finally spoke. "We're both just taking in what Emily shared with us."

"I can understand that." Abigail spoke up. "It's a lot to take in since you've been trying to prove this for a while now."

"Would you give us Penelope's information so we can contact her? Maybe thank her for the photo." Heidi asked. "I mean it's nice to have a photo of her and Edward Dalton, but we would like to meet her in person. Peter especially."

Piper held up his hand to motion to the others he would answer their question. "I made sure Penelope had your information so it would be her decision whether or not she wanted to contact you."

"What do you mean? We can't meet her or talk to her?" Peter asked. "What if we need her to back us up when we confront Joseph Wright?"

"Penelope wanted it to be her choice." Matthew interrupted. "We have to honor her request."

"Matthew's right." Piper interrupted. "She came to us in good faith to share her story. We made a promise to Penelope we would give her the choice of whether or not to meet with you."

"There has to be a way we can make her talk to us. I mean, after all, she's where all this started." Peter's voice sounded very annoyed.

Abigail tilted her head and glanced at Matthew with a startled look on her face.

"I think that's up to Penelope." Abigail spoke. "Like Matthew and Piper explained before, it's her choice how she wants to deal with what happened in her past."

"I think what Peter is trying to say is we might need her to prove what we are saying is the truth." Heidi's voice had a sound of desperation.

"We gave you all the information we have from the DNA results." Emily explained. "It should be enough for you to give to your lawyer who can give it to Joseph Wright and prove to him beyond a shadow of a doubt, you are his son."

There was silence in the room. Matthew, Abigail, Emily, and Piper exchanged glances around the table as they waited for a reply from Heidi and Peter. Abigail mouthed *perfect* to Emily and winked.

"I'd really like Peter to get to know all of the members of his biological family. Penelope would be one of those people." Heidi paused. "Are you sure there's no way you'll give us her contact information?"

"Sorry, Heidi," Piper replied. "A promise in our book is solid. From the beginning, all of us have honored the wishes of the other people involved. There were people Emily wanted to meet that wouldn't share their information with her. We have to think it's for the best."

188

"If Peter wrote her a letter telling her how much he would like to meet her and get to know her, would you be able to get it to her?" Heidi asked.

"I could do that," Piper replied. "Just send it to my office and I'll make sure it gets to her."

"I guess that's all we can ask for."

Piper could hear the disappointment in Heidi's voice. "I hope you understand, we have to respect Penelope's wishes. If it hadn't been for her coming to me and telling me her story, we wouldn't have the information we have now."

Abigail tried to make out what Peter and Heidi were saying as their whispers came over the phone. She could tell Peter wasn't happy with the fact he couldn't get his way and have Penelope's contact information.

"Piper's right. You guys owe all of this to Penelope. The information we could give you was enough to prove you belonged to the Dalton line, Peter, but Penelope added the missing piece you've been looking for. I think, at the very least, we owe it to her to make sure her request is honored."

"Yes, you're right, Abigail." Heidi hesitantly spoke. "I'll make sure we get a letter to you Piper in the next few days. If you could make sure Penelope receives it, please."

"I can do that." Piper offered.

"Thank you for calling. Peter and I will contact you if we have any questions about anything at all. It was good to talk to all of you." Heidi ended the call.

"Well, that went well." Piper smiled and rubbed the back of his neck.

"We didn't give them what they wanted. We're going to have to do everything we can to protect Penelope from Peter and Heidi." Abigail glanced around the table. "I have a feeling they're not done trying to find her."

CHAPTER TWENTY-ONE

"Wow. You look beautiful." Piper stepped back to get a better look at Lydia. Her red blouse set off the dark hair cascading down past her shoulders. The slacks she was wearing accentuated her perfect figure.

"Thanks, Piper." Lydia smiled. "You don't look bad yourself."

"This old thing." Piper ran his hand down his favorite navy-blue shirt. "It's just something I threw on."

"Well, it looks really nice on you. It sets off your eyes." Lydia motioned for him to come in. "Let me grab my jacket and we can go."

Piper stepped inside the door. Lydia's house was just about what he expected. Her decorating was more modern than her grandmother, Penelope's house. He wasn't an expert, but his idea of décor was drab compared to Lydia's.

"I have something for your grandmother. Would you mind if we stopped by before we go to dinner?" Piper asked.

"That would be fine. Let me call her and let her know we are on our way." Lydia took her cell out of her pocket and dialed. "Hi Grandmother. Listen, if you're not busy, Piper's here and has something for you. He would like to deliver it to you before we go to dinner."

Piper could here Penelope's voice coming over the phone. Lydia was smiling and nodding. He assumed that meant it would be all right.

"We'll see you in a few minutes." Lydia ended the call and placed her cell back in her pocket. "She's just watching television. She said she would love it if we stopped by so she could say hello to you."

"If you're ready, we can go then." Piper began walking toward the door. Lydia followed behind, locking it as she pulled it shut. "My grandmother's quite the fan of yours."

Piper smiled as he waited for Lydia. "She's a wonderful woman. It took a lot of courage for her to tell me her story. There aren't many women who would share what she did with a perfect stranger."

"My grandmother's a very good judge of character. If she would've had an ounce of reservation about you when she was in your office, she would not have hesitated to walk out on you."

Piper tilted his head as he opened the car door for Lydia then made his way around to the driver's side. Sliding behind the wheel, he started the engine.

"I've always envied people with that type of skill. Abigail's one of those people. She can read you like a book the moment she meets you. I always thought it came from her talent as a writer, but now I'm questioning that." Piper glanced at Lydia. "I can imagine that was fun for you growing up. Your friends and boyfriends meeting Penelope."

"Oh, believe me. There were some awkward moments. As you've learned, Grandmother doesn't hold back when she has an opinion. She wouldn't hurt anyone on purpose, but she could make someone extremely uncomfortable. Especially the boys I dated." Lydia shook her head.

"I'd love to hear some of those stories," Piper said.

"That will be dinner conversation." Lydia pointed out the window. "We're here."

****

"Hi, Grandmother." Lydia gave Penelope a hug as she stepped inside the front door.

"Penelope." Piper smiled. "It's good to see you again."

"You too, Samuel." Penelope reached for a hug. "I'm so glad to see the two of you going out on a date. It makes me very happy."

Piper looked to Lydia and caught her raising an eyebrow at him. He knew she was referencing their conversation on the car ride. He reached in his jacket pocket and took out an envelope and handed it to Penelope. "This is for you."

"What's this?" Penelope examined the blank envelope.

"It's a letter to you from Peter and Heidi Collins." Piper held up his hands. "Before you shoot the messenger, they wanted to meet with you. Abigail, Matthew, Emily, and I agreed we shouldn't share your information without your permission. We know how you felt about meeting them. So as a consolation, we agreed to bring you a letter they wrote saying whatever it was they wanted to say to you in person. This is that letter." Piper pointed to the envelope in Penelope's hands.

"You don't have to read it. You can tear it up, you can burn it, you can chop it up in the garbage disposal. Whatever you wish. I just promised to deliver it to you. I didn't promise you would read it."

"Have you read it or did they tell you what they wrote?" Penelope looked directly at Piper as she waited for his reply.

"No. It was sealed in an envelope addressed to my office. I took it out exactly like that." Piper motioned to the envelope. He watched as Penelope continued to examine the envelope, holding it up to the light to see if she could make out any writing. "It's completely up to you what you do with it." Piper repeated himself.

Penelope folded the envelope in half and placed it in her sweater pocket. "I'll have to think about this."

"I understand," Piper said. "I really used it as an excuse to see you again."

Penelope smiled at Piper. "Samuel Piper, you know you don't have to have a reason to stop by and see me. I'm happy to see you anytime at all."

"I'm hungry, if you're ready to go." Lydia winked at Piper. "I think my grandmother is hitting on my date."

"I'm ready," Piper laughed. "It was good to see you again Penelope." Piper gave her a quick hug.

"You two have a nice dinner and remember, Samuel, you can stop by anytime at all."

"Thank you, Penelope."

"I'll call you tomorrow, Grandmother." Lydia gave her grandmother a hug.

"You two make me very happy." Penelope smiled and waved as she closed the door behind them.

"You're right about Penelope saying exactly what's on her mind." Piper grinned, opening the car door for Lydia then walking around to the driver's side to climb in.

"Oh, just wait until you get to know her as well as I do." Lydia closed her car door.

"I've heard that comes with age. The saying exactly what's on your mind," Piper said.

"Grandmother has been that way since I've known her. Age has nothing to do with her frankness." Lydia explained.

"I'm a huge fan of saying what's on your mind." Piper nodded. "That way you know exactly where you stand with that person."

"Good." Lydia turned to Piper as he closed his car door. "I'm not really a nurse. I'm an exotic dancer at the local gentlemen's club."

Piper studied Lydia's face. Her expression was serious. Not knowing her long enough to tell where she was going with this, he wasn't sure how to handle the situation. He couldn't even think of a smartass remark.

"I guess if that's your thing." Piper stuttered.

Lydia suddenly broke out in laughter as she pointed a finger at him. "I'm sorry, but you should see the look on your face."

"That's not funny," Piper shook his head.

"It is too." Lydia was still laughing. "You said you like people who say what's on their mind because you knew where you stood with them. I was just testing you."

"I can tell I have a lot to learn about you." Piper put the car in reverse and began backing out the driveway. "Do you have your cell phone handy?"

Reaching in her pocket, she took out her cell and held it up in the air. "It's right here. Why?"

"Do you see that white car parked on the side of the road behind us?" Piper continued to look in the rearview mirror.

Turning her head, Lydia said, "Yes."

"Would you take a photo of it. Try and make sure you get the license plate."

"Got it." Lydia turned back and checked the photos she had taken. "What's up with the car?"

"Can you read the plate in the photo?"

"Yes. It's pretty clear."

"Great. Thank you." Piper drove off slowly, watching in the rearview mirror as the car stayed parked on the side of the road a few houses down from Penelope's house. "The car's been following me since I left town. I thought it was just a coincidence until now."

"What do you think they want?" Lydia asked.

"If I'm right, I think they want to find out where your Grandmother lives. I have a feeling Peter and Heidi Collins have something to do with this."

"You don't think they would hurt Grandmother, do you?" Lydia reached across and grabbed Piper's arm.

"I don't want to scare you or Penelope, but I'm not sure what they want." Putting the car in reverse, Piper backed up to Penelope's driveway. "We're going to get out of the car and stay with your grandmother. I'm going to call the local police and have them check the plates then we can decide what to do. You might need to take your grandmother home with you tonight after they're gone until we can figure this out."

Lydia reached to open her car door.

Taking her arm before she climbed out. "Try to act like nothing's wrong. Don't look back at the car. Just walk straight to the door like we forgot something. We want them to stay right where they are until the police have time to talk to them."

Piper put his arm around Lydia's waist as they walked slowly toward Penelope's door. "Everything's going to be all right. Don't worry. I'll make sure of it."

CHAPTER TWENTY-TWO

"I'd like to know what the hell you two were possibly thinking." Piper rolled his chair closer, putting his elbows on the desk and interlocking his fingers as he waited for Heidi or Peter to say something. The looks on their faces weren't telling him anything he needed to know. Only that they looked like two children who'd been caught stealing cookies out of the cookie jar.

"Come on you two." Piper narrowed his eyes at them. "Give me something. Anything that makes me feel better about what I learned about you. You hired a private detective to find Penelope Johnson-Harris after Matthew, Abigail, Emily, and I told you we wanted to leave it up to her to decide if she wanted to meet with you. Why the hell would you do that?"

"You didn't give us a choice in that decision." Heidi finally spoke and then turned to look at Peter. "We feel she's important to our case against Joseph Wright. We might need her to back up our story when or if we ever meet with him."

"You have all the test results and information you need to go to Joseph Wright and prove Peter's his biological son. Leaving the decision up to Penelope if she wanted to meet you, was the best answer. It wasn't your decision." Piper leaned back in his chair and locked his gaze on the two of them as he took a breath to calm himself.

"We need all the proof we can get," Heidi replied. "We've given all the information we have to our lawyer, but having Penelope in person to back up our story makes it stronger."

Peter sat silent, staring out the office window behind Piper. The expression on his face hadn't changed since he sat down. "Can you tell me what you were thinking, Peter? Or are you going to let you mother speak for you?" Piper wanted to hear his side. He wanted Peter to explain to him exactly why he would go to such lengths to find Penelope. Piper had a feeling this was Peter's idea, not Heidi's.

"She's explaining the situation perfectly." Peter finally spoke without moving or looking at Piper.

"Again, you don't need Penelope to prove to Joseph Wright you're his biological son. You have all the proof you need in the test results Emily sent you. Penelope even gave you a picture of her and Edward Dalton. What more do you want from her?" There was no change in Peter's expression. "I've gotten to know her and she's a wonderful woman who would do anything in her power if she thought it would benefit the situation. There's nothing more she can do. All you're doing is causing her to relive painful memories. Is that your plan?"

"Painful memories?" Peter glared at Piper. "You mean I'm a painful memory for Penelope? She's never met me. She doesn't know anything about me. How could I be a painful memory? If she took the time to get to know me, she would realize I'm worth the time and effort."

Piper shook his head and took a deep breath so he didn't go off on Peter like he wanted. "Look, Peter. This story isn't all about you. Other people have a part in it and it's up to each one of those people to decide how they handle what they learn about themselves and others. Believe me, all of us have learned that the hard way."

Leaning forward in his chair and putting his arms on the desk in front of him, Piper continued. "You're going to have to give Penelope time. If she decides sometime in the future, she wants to meet you and get to know you, that would be her choice not yours and Heidi's. You're going to have to realize you can't force the situation."

Heidi put her hand on Peter's arm to stop him from speaking. "We're not trying to force anything. What we both want is what Peter has coming to him and that would be for Joseph Wright to accept him as his son."

"You have everything you need to do that," Piper repeated himself.

"Penelope would be a wonderful addition to the information we have. She would be the one thing that seals the deal." Heidi glanced at Peter who returned to staring out the office window, not looking directly at anyone. "Isn't that right, Peter?"

Taking a few seconds before he answered, Peter turned his gaze to Piper and finally spoke. "I decided a long time ago that the people who deserve to share my life are the people who want the best for me. My mother and adopted father are two of those people. Penelope Johnson-Harris not wanting to meet me or take the time to get to know me shows me she doesn't deserve my attention."

"Don't you have any understanding for what Penelope has been through?" Piper asked through gritted teeth. "I mean she was left on her own and pregnant at a young age by Edward Dalton, your grandfather who'd forced himself on her. Her parents threatened to disown her if she kept her child. She couldn't take care of the child alone so the only thing she could do was give the child up. She did what she did thinking of that child first."

Heidi looked down at her hands nervously moving in her lap. Peter continued to look out the window.

"She found the courage to come forward to help us find the connection that brought all of us together and to thank her you don't give her the time and space she needs? Instead you hire a private detective to hunt her down like she's a criminal."

"That wasn't the reason at all." Heidi spoke softly.

"Then what was the reason? I don't understand how you couldn't consider Penelope's feelings instead of your own." Piper waited for either of they to reply.

"We..." Heidi was interrupted by Peter.

"It's not her choice." Peter exclaimed. "She's one of the ways I'm going to prove to Joseph Wright I'm his son."

"She's also your grandmother!" Anger filled Piper's response. "You need to start treating her with the respect she deserves. She's not just your proof, she's a person. A caring, loving person who has feelings. You're going to leave Penelope alone. Do you understand what I'm saying?"

"We understand." Heidi stood and pulled Peter's arm wanting him to stand. "I think we should go now. Come on, Peter."

Reluctantly standing, Peter joined her. "Penelope will regret her decision not to have anything to do with me."

"Leave Penelope out of this, Peter." Piper walked around his desk and stood next to him. "I really don't want to have to make that point any clearer to you. You come near her and you'll have to answer to me."

Heidi took Peter's arm and they both walked out of the office door without as much as a goodbye. Piper stayed right where he was. The farther away from Heidi and Peter Collins he was, the better off they were.

CHAPTER TWENTY-THREE

"You and Emily were right about Peter Collins." Piper picked up the coffee cup Martha had just placed in front of him and took a drink.

"There was something about him I noticed the first time we met him and Heidi. I couldn't explain it at the time, but it really bothered me." Abigail took a bite of her French fry as she bounced Archer on her knee. His attention was focused on something outside the window of the Puckerbrush Café.

"Tell us what happened." Matthew asked as he took a bite of his burger. "He must've really made you mad."

"Pissed me off is more like it. He's an arrogant little shit who needs to be taken down a few notches." Piper shook his head and sighed. "Sorry, Archer."

"I've never heard you talk about anyone like that before." Martha laughed as she placed Piper's burger on the table in front of him. She put her hand on his shoulder. "He must be a real piece of work."

"Oh, he is." Piper looked up at Martha. "He needs to go to one of your classes on how to act like an adult, Martha. You could teach him a few things."

"If you think it would help, I'd be happy to do just that." Martha offered.

"From the way Piper talks, it might be too late." Abigail ran her hand over Archer's head. "You have to start young and I don't think Heidi had it in her to teach Peter how to respect his elders."

"The man has no respect for anyone except himself." Piper shook his head.

"I hope he got your point to leave Penelope alone." Matthew added. "I would hate for her to be afraid he'll show up at her front door at any time."

"I don't think Penelope's afraid at all he'll show up. Lydia and I are the ones who are worried about that. So much so, that she's staying with Penelope for a few days until Lydia's parents show up for a planned visit just to make sure." Piper explained.

"Is Penelope all right with that?" Abigail asked.

"She resisted at first. Penelope's a pretty tough lady, but Lydia was able to convince her it was for the best. It'll be nice when Lydia's parents arrive. She still owes me a date."

"You should see your face light up when you talk about Lydia." Abigail winked at Martha who was still standing beside Piper.

"I can see the glow all the way from up here." Martha laughed.

"All right, you two. Stop right there." Piper held one hand in the air.

"Tell us about Lydia. It sounds like the two of you are getting to know each other better." Abigail watched Piper's face as his smile grew larger.

Martha took a seat next to Piper at their table. "Yes, tell us all about her. You have to agree it's better than talking about Peter Collins."

"You're right about that, but don't you have some apple pies to make?" Piper turned and asked Martha.

"Nope. I already took care of that this morning. I always have time to talk to you boys about your love lives." Martha laughed as she patted Piper's hand.

"Apple pie!" Matthew exclaimed. "I knew there was something I forgot to order."

"You didn't think I was going to let you leave without a piece of pie, did you?" Martha asked. "I'll get you one as soon as Piper tells us all about Lydia."

"The woman has her priorities." Abigail tilted her head and glanced at Martha.

"You guys aren't going to let me leave until I fill you in on everything, are you?" Piper glanced around the table. Everyone's heads were nodding. "Fine."

"Don't leave anything out." Martha moved closer to Piper so she didn't miss a word.

"Fine." Piper put his hands against the table and sat back in his chair. "Lydia and I were supposed to go to dinner the other night, but we ended up spending the evening at Penelope's because of Peter and Heidi's stupid idea. We have a good time together. I'm learning she has a great sense of humor. She makes me laugh. If we ever get to go out, just the two of us, I'm sure we'll have a good time."

"Make sure you keep us posted. You know your love life is important to us." Martha patted his hand as she stood. "I've got to get back to the kitchen and check on John and Charles. Those two get involved in a conversation and forget what they're doing. Make sure you don't leave without saying goodbye."

"My pie." Matthew held a finger in the air.

212

"I'll get it right now. A slice for everyone coming up." Martha disappeared into the kitchen.

"It won't be long before Archer will be able to share pie with you." Abigail smiled at Matthew as Archer made a cooing noise at the mention of his name.

"What's that?" Matthew cupped his hand around his ear and moved closer to Archer. "You'd rather share Mommy's apple pie? I think she wouldn't mind at all."

"Nice." Abigail nodded her head. "I can see no one, not even your son, is going to talk you out of a bite of your apple pie."

"I'll let you guys discuss whose pie Archer's going to share. I can tell you right now, it's not going to be mine. I've got to get back to the office." Piper stood from his chair, took his wallet out and placed money on the table by his plate. "I'll grab my apple pie on the way out."

"Maybe you should think about filing a restraining order against Peter and Heidi Collins. That might be a way to convince them to leave Penelope alone." Matthew suggested.

Piper nodded. "I could give that a try. Anything to make them think twice about attempting anything stupid again like the other night."

213

"Wait!" Martha yelled from across the café her arms flailing in the air.

"I was coming to get my pie, Martha. You don't have to bring it to me." Piper walk around the table to meet her.

"I thought of something when I was cutting each of you a piece of pie. You already have a solution to keeping Peter and Heidi away from Penelope." Martha appeared proud of herself for whatever it was she thought of.

"What do you mean Martha?" Piper asked.

"Lydia." Martha patted Piper's arm. "You have Lydia. She's Penelope's granddaughter so Joseph Wright is her uncle. You're Edward Dalton's grandson so Joseph Wright is also your uncle. Together you guys are proof Joseph Wright belongs in this family."

"You might have something there, Martha." Matthew commented.

"I think Martha's been reading too many Leeza McBride mysteries." Abigail laughed.

Piper gave Martha a hug. "Thanks Martha. I'll give Lydia a call and see if she is willing to meet a few distant relatives."

"It will give you a good reason to talk to her." Martha raised her eyebrows as she winked at Piper. "Let's go get you a piece of apple pie to go." She took his arm as they walked back toward the kitchen.

"Don't forget my pie." Matthew yelled behind them.

Martha held her free hand up in the air to acknowledge Matthew's request.

Archer made a loud cooing sound and smiled at Matthew.

"I'll have her bring you one too." Matthew leaned down and kissed Archer's forehead.

"I have my hands full with you two." Abigail smiled. "I wouldn't have it any other way."

CHAPTER TWENTY-FOUR

"You promised me there would be no way they would find me." Joseph Wright moved close to Martin Wright, staring into the old man's eyes as he waited for his reply.

"I did everything I could, Joseph. I made sure Edward Dalton's name wasn't on any legal document to do with the church a long time ago. There's no record of me adopting you. I also falsified the DNA sample so they couldn't prove the child in question was yours. I don't know how they got the information that led them to you."

Martin backed up and took a seat in the closest chair. He placed a hand on his chest as his heart was beating fast. It happened a lot lately. Was this God's way of making him face his sins? He knew what he did was wrong at the time. He did it out of love and was trying to protect Joseph, who was young and had a bright future in front of him. He wanted Joseph to take over the church because he possessed a way of bringing people to the Lord.

"Well, it's obvious you didn't do enough." Joseph brought Martin's thoughts back to the present. "According to their lawyer they have proof I'm this Peter Collins's biological father. Do you know what that means?" His tone filled with anger; Joseph waved clenched fists in the air.

Martin didn't say a word. He locked eyes with Joseph and waited for him to continue.

"Let me tell you what this means old man." Joseph shook the papers he held tightly. "This means, if we can't debunk their proof, Peter Collins stands to lay claim to part of everything I've worked hard for. Everything I've spent most of my life building. There's no way I'm giving any part of this church or my fortune to Peter Collins. I'll see him ruined first."

Martin watched Joseph's face turn beet red. His eyes grew larger than he'd ever seen. If he didn't calm down, Martin was afraid he would have a stroke or a heart attack. Joseph paced back and forth in front of his office desk slapping the pieces of paper against his leg, his Rolex reflecting glints of the sunshine coming through the stained-glass window. Martin hadn't kept up with Penelope Johnson. She had to be how Peter Collins found out about Martin. She was the only link left that would have any information about Joseph's parentage.

"I think you should meet with their lawyer and see what it is he wants before you jump to any conclusions, Joseph. Maybe he doesn't want anything except to know his biological father." Martin finally spoke trying to keep the tone of his voice calm and soothing. "You're not going to know for sure what he wants until you meet with him."

Joseph paced back and forth in front of Martin for the next few minutes. He stopped and took a breath. "I'll make sure our lawyers stall them as long as they can. When it's no longer possible, I won't have a choice except to meet with this Peter Collins."

"Joseph, you've done a wonderful job of growing this church and you have so much to show for it. You have a beautiful home. You've given me and your mother a beautiful home which we are very grateful for. You drive an expensive car and your clothes are all tailored for you. There's really nothing else you need. Don't you think meeting your biological son could enrich your life? Maybe give you something that you never knew you needed?" Martin knew trying to reason with Joseph didn't always work, but it was worth trying.

"Enrich my life?" Joseph leaned against the edge of his desk as he threw his head back and laughed. He dropped his head and stared at Martin. The amusement on his face disappeared. "He can ruin me. Not only me, but everything I've built. If this gets out, the fact I have an illegitimate child, we'll lose parishioners and when we lose parishioners, we lose tithes, when we lose tithes, we lose the ability to afford our homes, my cars, my clothes. I was planning to add a private jet to my collection. I can't and won't let him ruin me."

Joseph walked around his desk and sat down in his chair interlocking his fingers in front of him.

Martin recognized his expression. It was the one expression he had which most resembled Edward Dalton. Martin knew what was happening. Joseph was internalizing his thoughts, plotting in an attempt to find a way out of this situation, trying to find someone else to blame. This is when Martin began to worry. Joseph was an intelligent man, but he also possessed a vindictive, evil side which showed its ugly face when he became cornered. These were traits Martin recognized Joseph inherited from his biological father, Edward Dalton.

As Joseph was growing up, Martin and his wife tried to talk to him, help him through situations he would get himself into so the traits wouldn't surface. If they did, he would have the tools to control them. They prayed for him and with him, attempting to give him an outlet to work out his frustration.

This time Martin didn't know how to help him. If Joseph wouldn't listen to him when it came to Peter Collins, there was nothing he could do. Martin sat up in his chair.

"Joseph, when I took you in after your biological mother left you at the church, I didn't worry about providing for you or worry about what I would have to give up because of you. I knew the Lord would give me what I needed to provide for you. All I had to do was give you the love you deserved. The love every child deserves. Your mother and I have done the best we could. Maybe you should look at Peter that way. You don't have any children of your own, except for Peter. If you give him a chance, maybe just maybe, he can provide for you." Martin paused for a few seconds to take stock of whether Joseph was listening to him or not. He did his best to read Joseph's expression. Martin could tell Joseph was listening. He may not be responding, but he was listening.

"You're going to need someone who can take over the church when you decide to step aside, Joseph. Just like you took over for me. There's no one now who can take your place. No one as good as you are with people. Turning them toward the Lord. Preaching God's word so people understand. Peter might be just the person you need. You can train him, teach him, show him the way of the Lord. You can do it. I know you can."

Joseph finally looked at Martin. "You think I should meet with him?"

"I do." Martin smiled. "If he's your son, you'll know and he'll have inherited your drive and determination to make a success of the church by following in your footsteps."

"After the news gets out to the congregation, it'll be hard for me to bring him into the church and have the congregation accept him. It'll also do harm to my reputation. I can't have that. I can't take the chance of having my reputation tarnished."

"Not if what the congregation's told is Peter Collins is joining the Wright Way Church as a preacher. The private agreement between you and Peter could be that he remains Peter Collins to the congregation, not your son, so the damage to the church and your reputation would be minimal."

Martin could see in Joseph's eyes and expression; he was considering Martin's suggestion. Maybe, once again, Martin found a solution to the situation Joseph was in. Maybe the Lord had provided an answer.

CHAPTER TWENTY-FIVE

The congregation of the Wright Way Church began filling the sanctuary as soon as the doors were opened, finding their seats among the pews. Little children skipping down the aisle behind their parents, neighbors greeting neighbors, friends greeting friends as talk and laughter filled the air. The tight-knit family was growing larger every Sunday.

Televising the services was one of the best ideas Joseph felt he had since he took over the church. It not only brought in members, but it made him well-known around town making it hard for him to go anywhere without a request for prayer or blessing of some kind.

It was the ushers' job to control the crowd so when the cameras began filming, everyone would already be seated and quiet.

Joseph Wright paced the floor of his office as he prepared himself for the service. He'd worked all week on his sermon for tonight. This was a special one. The subject was trust. He needed to plant the seed so when he introduced Peter Collins, the members of the congregation would be accepting. The parents needed to trust Peter Collins and the children needed to accept him enough so they would allow him to get close.

Bringing new preachers into the fold was a very delicate process. They had to be groomed to look, feel, and think like what Joseph believed was Christian. Any character flaw which members of the flock might find offensive or distasteful needed to be eradicated. When they were in the presence of members of the church, their appearance should be immaculate, the tone of their voice pleasing, their conversation centered around the good of the church, and the work of the Lord. Anything less wouldn't be accepted.

"I need to check your mic." One of the assistants interrupted Joseph's thoughts.

"Come in." Joseph waved his hand as he let out a sigh of disgust. He stood in place as the young girl inspected the wire running up the back of his shirt to an earpiece with a microphone attached to the end.

"We need a mic check." The assistant spoke into her headset.

"Testing one, two, three." Joseph spoke in a normal voice into the microphone.

"Everything's working fine. Whenever you're ready, just let them know." The young girl turned and walked out the office door.

Joseph closed his eyes and took a few deep breaths trying to return to the zone where he needed to be so he could bring the flock to their knees as they opened their wallets. He knew he needed at least five minutes of quiet so he could enter the trance-like state required for him to preach the word the way it was intended. The way he needed to preach it in order to keep the membership growing and the money flowing in.

"I'm ready. I'll be on stage in one minute. Make sure Peter Collins is ready for me to introduce him." Joseph spoke into the microphone as he made his way out his office door and down the hallway to the sanctuary entrance.

He walked past the few people standing in the hallway without speaking a word. The crew of the church production team were under strict instructions not to speak to him or in any way acknowledge him when he was making his way to the pulpit; not wanting to bring him out of his trance. Several employees were fired for as little as a sneeze when he walked by.

Joseph stopped in the doorway of the sanctuary, took another deep breath and said a prayer Martin had always said before stepping out in front of the crowd. *Lord help me to spread your word and open the hearts of all those in need. Amen.*

The pews were full as Joseph looked out over the crowd. He smiled a smile large enough to be seen from the back of the room. He knew the television loved him. He could feel the eyes of the congregation in the room on him and the eyes of the people watching at home. It was a feeling he thrived on. One that was hard to describe. It was like a power surging through his body that didn't leave until he'd finished for the evening. It was a high like nothing he'd ever felt before. He stepped into the spotlight.

"Praise the Lord. Praise the Lord." Joseph spoke as he raised his arms in the air letting the congregation know it was time to begin. The crowd erupted in amen and hallelujah.

"I'm so glad you all could be here tonight. This is a very special night for the Wright Way Church." Joseph strode back and forth in front of the crowd. "I would like to take a few moments before we begin the service to introduce a new member of our church." He stepped back and placed his hand on the shoulder of Peter Collins. "This young man has come to me very highly recommended. You could say he's a member of the family." Joseph smiled and winked at Peter.

The younger man moved forward and waved at the audience, then stepped back out of the spotlight.

Joseph continued, "I'd like all of you in the congregation to welcome Peter Collins. I want you to stop and say hello to Peter after today's service, introduce yourself, especially all the teenagers out there. Peter's going to become our new youth pastor. I know each of you will want to get to know him personally and all you parents will want to know exactly what kind of person will be leading your children to find their place with the Lord. Peter will have such a great influence over your children, so make him feel welcome."

C. DEANNE ROWE

C. Deanne Rowe was born and raised in southwest Oklahoma. She has also lived in Nebraska, Texas, and California. Iowa has been her home for over thirty years where she lives with her husband, two children and their spouses, five grandchildren, and her hero teacup toy poodle, Allie.

She has always loved writing poetry and short stories and became a published romance author later in life. She has published eight books of her own, three in her *Valley* series, four in her *Cowboy Temptation* series and one non-fiction. As one of the Stiletto Girls with Magnolia 'Maggie' Rivers and Glenna West, she is an author of ten novellas in the *Stiletto Girls* series.

You can find additional information about her other writing on her websites:

www.comfortedfromheaven.com
www.cdeannerowe.com
www.thestilettogirls.com

Other books in the Puckerbrush Series: